Abou

Douglas Bruton has been published in various publications including *Northwords Now*, *New Writing Scotland*, *Aesthetica* and *The Irish Literary Review*. His short stories have won competitions including Fish and the Neil Gunn Prize. He has had two novels published, *The Chess Piece Magician* and *Mrs Winchester's Gun Club*.

Blue Postcards

DOUGLAS BRUTON

Fairlight Books

First published by Fairlight Books 2021

Fairlight Books
Summertown Pavilion, 18–24 Middle Way, Oxford, OX2 7LG

A CIP catalogue record for this book is available from the
British Library

1 2 3 4 5 6 7 8 9 10

ISBN 978-1-912054-77-0

www.fairlightbooks.com

Printed and bound in Great Britain by Clays Ltd.

Designed by Sara Wood

Illustrated by Sam Kalda

For A

I

Tekhelet Threads

1. At the foot of the steps of *Le Passage de la Sorcière* in Montmartre sits a man in a blue suit, the sleeves of his jacket pushed up to his elbows, his shirt collar unfastened and his blue tie loose around his neck. He sits playing with three chased silver egg cups and a wooden ball the size of a pea. He asks passers-by if they would like to bet on which egg cup the ball is under, after he does a dance of the cups, shifting the order and showing the wooden ball and then not showing it. It is a trick of course, but he does it so well it's hard to see how. Once I saw him lift all three cups and there was no ball at all; it had disappeared.

2. He's a showman and he makes everything look easy. He feigns surprise when the ball is not where it should be and he laughs, showing gaps in his yellow teeth when he does and one tooth has a blue stone fixed in it.

3. Maybe he doesn't sit there now. Maybe he has disappeared for there are gendarmes in blue-black uniforms and pillbox hats, and they move people along if they are causing a disturbance.

4. Years ago in the blue mists of memory, there was a street in Paris called the Street of Tailors. Men sat outside their shops like kings on their thrones, and they nodded to each other or tipped their broad-brimmed hats and said, 'Shalom,' and smiled.

8

There were also dressmakers on that street and gentlemen's outfitters and cloth merchants. Then one day the whole street disappeared and all the people in it.

5. Now that street has a different name, though there is a tailor there and he wears a shawl some days, fringed with tassels. Four of the tassels each have, according to the law written in his book, a blue thread running through them. The man's name is Henri and he works in the shop, taking down the measurements of men's inside legs and the width of their shoulders and the thickness of their waists. He writes all these measurements down in a leather-bound ledger that is kept locked in a safe as though it is a book of secrets.

6. I remember standing at a stall beside the Eiffel Tower. The sky was so blue it hurt to look at it. I stopped by the stall because it offered shade from an awning that stretched above three fold-down tables. On one table there were boxes of postcards in some sort of arrangement. They were old postcards – pictures of Paris over the years. I leafed through them, idly, in order to justify my sheltering. One card caught my eye.

7. It was a blue postcard. Completely blue on one side, a blank and eternal blue – though the paper was a little yellowed and cracked and

the corners of the card rounded. On the reverse side, on the left, the postcard had a message in French, on the right a name and address. It carried a stamp in the top right-hand corner, a stamp that was completely blue; it had been franked and was dated 14 May 1957. I do not think the girl serving at the stall knew what she had. It was priced at one euro.

8.   It is not easy to escape the drag and pull of time; its laws are pretty specific. And in the end a life lived is soon forgotten. My father, for example: all that's left of him now are stories I tell to my children, and telling them over and over they shift, a little each time, so I am not sure how much they are true. And when I say, 'Now the street has a different name and there is a tailor there,' what does that 'now' signify, for he is not there as I write this but was there once, a long time ago, before I was born even. I was born on 14 May 1957. It is a small coincidence that the date of my birth is the date stamped on the reverse side of the blue postcard and it is not that fact that made me purchase the card.

9.   There was a time when the colour blue was reserved for paintings of the Madonna, her shawl or her dress. The ultramarine pigment seemed to burn on the canvas. It was obtained

from a mineral, derived from the crushing of lapis lazuli. At one point in history that came from one mine in the furthest reaches of Afghanistan. It travelled west along the Silk Road, wrapped in cloth and tucked under the clothes of dark-skinned merchants. It was worth more than gold then and so it could only be used for pictures of the most holy.

10. Lapis blue is a colour that seems to stand the test of time. The varnish that is layered over the top yellows with age, but conservators can strip that old varnish away and underneath the blue still burns with the intensity of flame.

11. The man shifting egg cups sitting at the bottom of the steps at *Le Passage de la Sorcière* in Montmartre – when he has not been moved on by the gendarmes and when we are in the right time, his time – has that blue stone in his tooth, a polished piece of lapis lazuli.

12. At some point in the nineteenth century a process was developed for the production of an artificial ultramarine blue and artists were no longer dependent on the expensive lapis lazuli.

13. Henri the tailor wears a suit when he is at work. He wears a tie also, with a pin, and he smiles more than he does when he is not working.

The men who visit the shop where he works know him by name and they pass the time of day – his day – with him, remarking on the price of bread now the war is only a memory or making comment as to the colour of girls' dresses that once were dull and grey and now are like rainbows. They shake cigarettes out of blue soft packs and they stand stiffly like shop mannequins, one arm outstretched so Henri can measure the length of the sleeve. And Henri is permitted to hold their fingers in his and to stroke their broad backs with the flat of his palm and to run his hand, soft and slow as a caress, up their inside legs.

14. The girl at the postcard stall beside the Eiffel Tower asks me if I want a bag for the blue postcard and she smiles. She says she has red postcards, too, and green and yellow, and the shape of her lips when she speaks is the shape of kisses. I accept her offer of a bag and she slips my blue postcard into a brown paper envelope.

15. It is a fact that colour perception deteriorates with age, particularly in the area of the spectrum that covers blue, blue-greens and yellows. I worry about that in a way that I never worried about the deterioration of hearing – there are high-pitched sounds that adolescents hear and that are

beyond the reach of adults after around the age of twenty-five. Some security firms use this high pitch in alarms fitted to buildings where teenagers and anti-social behaviour are a problem. It never worried me that I could not hear the high mosquito-whine of those alarms; but I worry that one day blue might not be blue when I look at it. Maybe that is why I collect things that are blue and surround myself with them.

16. One of my favourite paintings is Van Gogh's *Wheatfield with Crows*. It is one of his last paintings. The yellow of the cornfield is aflame and the blue of the sky is a dark and brooding glory. I saw it hanging in the Van Gogh Museum in Amsterdam; it took my breath away and I wanted to step into the painting. It would be an unimaginable loss not to see that blue or that yellow in the way I see it now. It would be a loss comparable to the loss of words and thoughts.

17. Her name is Michelle, the girl at the postcard stall beside the Eiffel Tower. It says so on a handwritten badge pinned to her blouse. She holds the brown paper envelope out to me and it is one of those moments when an old man wishes he was young again, wishes he was back in '*l'époque bleue*', when a boy could hear all the sounds in the world and see all the colours fresh.

18. If Henri is following the laws in his book to the letter, then the blue twisted thread that is in each of the four tassels on his shawl should be a colour that is described as Tekhelet. It is a particular colour of blue: the pure blue of the clear noonday sky; it represents the eternal and the presence of the divine. Henri does not know all of this. He understands that the blue thread is lucky, that is all, and that is why it appears as though he keeps to the law as laid down in the book.

19. I have a stone on my windowsill. It is small enough it can fit in my mouth, though no words can fit in there along with it. Maybe it is lucky and maybe it is blue. In the sun it looks grey but if I lick it wet then it is blue. When it dries it is grey again.

20. I think my father's eyes were blue. I think they were. I am not sure.

21. My hand shakes when I take the postcard in its brown bag. I thank Michelle, not by name; that is something I say only in my head. My hand shakes not because her eyes are blue, like I think my father's were, nor because her lips when she speaks make kisses in the air. My hand shakes because I know what the blue postcard is and I

cannot believe I have purchased it for only one euro. It feels like cheating, like I am breaking the law somehow. And she is so pretty I almost tell her, but the words are lost or merely in my head somewhere.

22. When I turn away from the girl called Michelle, I check in the bag. I once bet on an egg cup at the bottom of the steps at *Le Passage de la Sorcière* in Montmartre, bet on a wooden ball being under it, and the man with the blue stone in his tooth asked me to lift the cup and he said to do it with a flourish, making a big reveal. I did it just the way he said and there was no ball there and he laughed and pocketed my money. So, when I turn my back to Michelle, I quietly check to make sure that the blue postcard is there in the brown bag.

23. Is it cheating if my father's eyes were not blue and I now imagine them blue? My eyes are blue and so I think his eyes must have been blue, but I do not really know.

24. Henri has a way of writing men's names in the ledger. He uses an old blue Bayard Excelsior fountain pen – '*le stylo sans reproche*'. He keeps the lever-fill pen clipped to his inside jacket pocket. The pen is always filled with Super Encre manufactured by Clio. It is a blue-black ink and when he writes men's names in

the ledger he does so with a careful flourish at the end of the name, almost ornamental in its kick and swirl, a small hurrah.

25. Beside the stone on my windowsill is a shard of blue glass. It once was part of a window in a church. The church has gone now and no one even remembers that it was there. They did not save the windows, just pulled them down with the stone. I crept into the demolished church one night and rescued the blue piece of glass. The blue is maybe the end of a sleeve, for there is part of a hand sketched in dark brown on one edge of the glass, the fingers extended and elegant. I sometimes hold the glass over my eyes and look at the world not as it is but in cobalt blue.

26. The law says that the blue thread in Henri's shawl must be made from a dye extracted from a sea creature known as Hilazon or Chilazon. There is a sea snail (*Murex trunculus*) whose body exudes a dye that at first looks almost purple, but when the dyed cloth is exposed to light it undergoes a chemical change to blue – the right sort of blue. The population of this sea snail increases dramatically in cycles of seven years. Henri's book says something about taking the sea snail when they surface every seventy years – it is understood that 'seventy' is an error and the first scribe meant 'seven'.

27. It takes 10,000 sea snails to produce only a few grams of the blue dye.

28. Back in my apartment in rue Germain Pilon in Montmartre, I put on blue latex gloves to handle the card. I hold it up to the window to examine the blue surface, bright as light cutting through blue glass in a church window. It has been handled a lot. It is slightly water-stained and the card has ruffled a little and there are marks from a hundred fingers on the blue. On the reverse side the stamp interests me. It is the same blue as the card, just blue with nothing else, except the frank mark running over it. The card is addressed to someone called H. Hartung, 7 Rue Cels, Paris 14.

29. Yves Klein was a *mythomane*. He made up the stories of his life and changed them at will. It is the same when someone dies and their stories shift from the truth, and become shorter so they can be told at family gatherings over drinks and cake. Yves Klein cannot be trusted to tell the truth any more than the people who tell stories of the dead. It is Yves Klein's postcard that I hold in my hand, his blue stamp that is franked with the date of my birth and the card addressed to H. Hartung.

30. I have been to Nice only once. I was there with friends, a husband-and-wife couple. She was pregnant and could not manage the shelved shingle beach and the shifting water. She described herself as a landed whale and laughed at her predicament, laughed to hide that she was cross. He was a musician and he played guitar and wrote bad music. I recall that I had never seen a sky so blue as the sky above Nice and the buildings were made of a white stone on which the sunlight burned so fiercely that it was always like walking in fire. Yves Klein was born on the rue Verdi in Nice, the only child of bohemian artist parents. He knew painting in his crib. That's what he'd tell you.

31. Sometimes I wonder if going back to Nice I would find the sky so blue or if the blue that I found there back in 1981 had something to do with being young or something to do with memory.

32. We motored down from Nice to Monte Carlo in the late afternoon and ate *moules marinières* from battered tin plates in a backstreet café. I have never had mussels that tasted half so good. I kept one of the shells, blue and darkness and white, like the sea at night and the moon thrown down on the breaking water.

33. Sometimes the measure of a man alters. It is always best to check before cutting the cloth for a new suit. Henri leads the way through to the back of the shop. There's a curtained alcove there where men can undress, down to their underwear. Some come out still wearing their socks and their shoes. They look a little comical, Henri thinks, when they step out from behind the blue curtain and stand in the middle of the back room waiting for Henri's hand to run up their bare inside leg.

34. As a child Yves Klein was called 'Mouse' and he sometimes lived with 'Tantine', his Aunt Rose, and sometimes he lived with his parents and sometimes he was sent to school. His aunt in Nice was strict and orderly and told him stories of St Rita and how bees crawled into her open mouth when she lay sleeping in her cot and crawled out again leaving her unharmed. His parents were relaxed and free and sometimes in Paris; with them he could disappear for days if he chose, off into the blue. Yves Klein knew how to be one thing to his aunt and another to his parents. At school he was lazy and without focus.

35. St Rita is the patron saint of lost causes. She is sometimes the saint of the impossible. Once, it is said, she levitated, nothing between her

and the ground others walked on, nothing but blue air. Near the end of her life, when she was in pain from a thorn in her head and tuberculosis, she asked a visitor to fetch her a rose from a garden she had once frequented. It was January and a rose was not expected. When one was found, in full bloom, it was brought to Rita on her deathbed.

36.   None of these stories are to be trusted, for they are stories of the dead told by the living and the living always lie, white and blue lies. A 'blue lie' is a lie told for the collective good. Stories of saints and their miracles may be thought of as blue lies. Like white lies they mean no harm.

37.   I trap the blue postcard between two pieces of Perspex and some days I display it out of the sun, blue side up; on other days I turn it so I can see the blue stamp and the address of H. Hartung, 7 Rue Cels, Paris 14.

38.   Henri lays the fabric flat on a wide table. He has a man's measurements scribbled on a torn piece of notepaper and pinned to the table. He uses a tape measure and brown paper patterns to lay out the shape of the man on the cloth, adjusting the shape to fit the figures written down on the scrap of paper. He moves quickly and under his breath he hums music

to himself. He uses tailor's chalk to mark the cut and the line of the man's suit. The chalk is not strictly speaking chalk, but is made from talc and it is blue.

39. At the end of the day, when the lights are coming on all over Paris and the gendarme, who is kicking his heels beneath the Eiffel Tower, is thinking about his wife and what she will put on the table for his supper, Michelle packs away the boxes of postcards and the books and the CDs. She packs them away into the back of an old Peugeot 4DA van, circa 1952. Once it was blue, but by this time it has lost all its colour.

40. Not all French war stories have the boot and stamp of occupation on them. Yves Klein's parents survived and suffered only the discomfort of not having so much. Maybe they were a little thinner and their clothes hung loose about their bodies. Yves Klein, Mouse, survived also and he had a childhood of sorts and he went to school and his life was not turned on its head by the war. Skies are blue or grey or filled with cloud regardless.

41. I recall the exercise books we wrote in when we were in school. Their covers were blue and the pages were lined in blue with a red margin.

There was space on the cover for our names and the title of the class we were in and our teacher's name. They were not a nice blue, if I remember right. They were blue like ink stains that won't shift from the cuffs of boys' shirts or blue like old egg boxes or tram tickets.

42. Not blue like gaslight.

43. Not the blue of the sky over Nice that Yves Klein, one burning blue day, put his name to, conducting the infinite with the waving of his signature finger, as though the sky could be *his* artwork because he said it was.

44. Not the blue of sea running shallow over white sand or stone.

45. Henri these days does not pray to the blue infinite God, not these after-war days. Not after what happened and He must have let it happen. That's what Henri thinks and so he does not pray these days.

46. Michelle is missing when I retrace my steps next day to the stalls arranged in crooked lines near the Eiffel Tower. There is a space where her stall should be – like the space under the empty egg cup when I lifted it and there was no wooden pea-sized ball underneath and the

man with the blue stone in his tooth laughed and took my money. I ask the man at the next stall if he knows where she is. The man shrugs and looks away.

47. At the end of war the seventeen-year-old Yves Klein was thinking on what he would be as a man. He did not know. His parents were both artists and his mother was making a name for herself in the art world. Yves Klein wanted something more than that. He wanted blue ribbons and gold laurel crowns and rose petals strewn at his feet. He wanted only what the young always want, which is to say he wanted to stand taller than anyone ever stood before.

48. The 'Blue Riband' was once a prize awarded for the fastest crossing of the Atlantic Ocean by passenger liners.

49. Earlier than that the 'Cordon Bleu' was a blue ribbon worn by an order of knights.

50. The Americans changed the spelling – as they are wont to do – and the blue ribbon was awarded to those athletes who achieved first place in sporting events.

51. The first belt in Kodokan judo ranking is a light blue. Yves Klein thought that maybe judo

was where he could stand tall with the whole world thrown at his feet. He gave years to the study and even travelled to Japan, perhaps in search of authenticity.

52. Henri had always wanted to be a tailor. It is what his father had been and his grandfather before him. Once there had been a shop on a whole street of tailors and Henri had started there, started as a boy, his grandfather sitting on a wooden throne out front tipping his hat to the other cloth-kings in the street and his father teaching him how to sew with a machine that was powered by a foot pedal. Above that shop was the family name written in blue letters like cut pieces of the sky. The shop is there still, though the street has disappeared and Henri's father and grandfather are only stories he tells to himself when he is not humming music.

53. Sometimes a thread breaks and there is no picking up of that thread again. This does not happen much in books for it is considered bad writing to leave a thread hanging. Threads like that can unravel, the whole garment made ragged and its shape altered. The friends I was with in Nice, the woman who was pregnant and her husband who wrote bad music, they are like broken threads and I do not know where they are today. I do not know why I

have mentioned them here at all, except that I was writing of Yves Klein in Nice and I remembered them then, this husband and his big wife, just as I remembered how blue the sky was.

54. Michelle is not there again and the man at the next stall is counting twenty-euro notes into piles that he separates with elastic bands, counting them into blue hundreds and blue five hundreds. He shrugs and he interrupts his counting, says sometimes she is there and sometimes she is not. 'There's no pattern to her coming and going,' he says. The man asks if I am looking for anything specific. I shake my head and smile. He returns to his counting.

55. Yves Klein, even as he was ascending the judo rankings, produced works that he called paintings. A single colour filling a whole canvas – rose or orange or blue or red. He showed these works to friends but they did not understand and they looked thoughtful and serious, all the while expecting that there was a punchline that would reveal the joke.

56. I drink my tea from a blue fluted Royal Copenhagen teacup, circa 1900. It was produced at the Royal Porcelain Factory. The cup is white with a pattern of thin blue lines and dots and they look like flowers or the seed

heads of grasses. The cup was designed by the architect Arnold Krog. The pattern originally came from China. My fingers do not fit into the handle so I hold the bowl of the cup in the palms of my hands and that way I know if the tea is too hot or cold, or the right temperature for me to drink.

57. There is a blue porcelain saucer that goes with the cup but it is missing.

58. Henri cuts the cloth that will soon be a suit. He cuts it with a confidence that comes from years of cutting cloth. It looks like a magic trick when he does it, or a performance. He holds his breath from the moment the scissors bite until the cut is finished. His action might be thought something akin to prayer except that Henri no longer believes in prayer, even though he still wears his prayer shawl sometimes, fingering the tassels at the corners, twisting and untwisting the blue Tekhelet thread.

59. I take milk with my tea. If I am by myself I use a small Limoges *pot à lait*. I think maybe it has some value. It is a squat white milk jug with gold leaf and blue and pink flowers on the side. The blue flowers are, I believe, cornflowers; I do not know what the pink flowers are.

60. I take sugar in my tea. Two teaspoons of sugar. For the sugar I use a small vintage willow pattern bowl, made in Stoke-on-Trent, England. It is chipped on the rim but there is something in the shape and the colour of the blue willow pattern story, the blue birds almost kissing in flight, something in it that still charms after all these years.

61. My mother drank her coffee from the bowl I now use for sugar. That's what my father told me. He held the bowl as he said my mother did and lifted it to his kissing lips and mimed the silent drinking of coffee. Maybe it is just a story of his. I inherited the blue bowl after my father passed away.

62. I don't remember my mother except through the blue willow pattern stories my father told me.

63. The willow pattern tells the tale of a Mandarin's daughter – a story of forbidden love and the death of a daughter and her lover by her father's orders. It tells of two lovers turned to blue doves by the sympathetic gods. It is just an English soft story. It is a story manufactured to sell porcelain in the nineteenth century.

64. Yves Klein once said that it was very difficult to paint, more difficult than anyone could

imagine. He talked of the energy that is given to a painting by the artist and not just the energy but something else. He is a little vague on what this something else is but it is something holy and blue, like a force that is at first in the artist and then is taken out of the artist by the act of painting and is then in the painting.

65. Maybe she was there on days when I was not. I cannot know this. I only know that she was not there for the days that I was. Then one day – quite out of the blue as they say – she is there again. Michelle, wearing a badge with her name on and looking hopefully at anyone who stops to look in her boxes of books and postcards and CDs.

66. I had begun to question her existence or the details that I had saved of her in my memory. I had begun to doubt that her eyes were blue just as I have begun to doubt that my father's eyes were blue.

67. I do not think she recognises me. She smiles and asks if she can help. The man at the next stall recognises me; he waves a blue twenty-euro note at me and nods.

68. I ask Michelle if she has any more blue post-cards. I do not use her name, not yet. I hope by

saying that 'more' – any *more* blue postcards
– she will begin to remember me.

69. Time was something of interest to Yves Klein.
He made great pronouncements on time to his
friends. He declared once that time would soon
be conquered, that one day there would be no
past or blue future but only an infinite present.

70. Henri pins the separate pieces of the suit
together. Drapes them over a leather mannequin that he has adjusted so it is nearer to
the size and shape of the man whose suit it
will be. He has cut interfaces and facing, and
he fixes some of these to the wool so that the
jacket begins to hang like a jacket should. He
holds the pins between the press of his lips so
he cannot speak, but he still makes the sound
of blue music, in pieces.

71. She directs me to a box that, when I look
in it, I see contains old Victorian postcards
showing half-dressed women with their hair
down and gazing at the camera, looking with
a masquerade want and hunger in their eyes,
their breasts showing. Some have no clothes on
at all and they are brushing their hair or letting
diaphanous cloth fall from their outstretched
legs or they are admiring flowers in a vase and
are unaware that they are naked and seen. This

is the 'blue' Michelle thinks I mean and so I know she does not remember me.

72. When he landed in Japan, Yves Klein was no longer a novice in respect of judo. He was far beyond the beginners' blue belt. He visited the venerable Kodokan Institute in Tokyo, but they would not accept the testimony of his French paperwork and so he had to begin all over again.

73. In this infinite present that Yves Klein talked of, I do not know if the past and future simply would no longer exist or if past and future would exist now as present. If all time existed together like this then my mother and father would still be sitting at the table in the kitchen, my mother drinking coffee from a willow pattern bowl and my blue-eyed father drinking in every detail of her – the way her hair fell across her face and without thinking she reached up and with the index finger of her right hand she brushed that miscreant curl of hair back behind her ear in an action that my father would turn into poetry when he told me of it, or turns into poetry even as he is telling me, even as it is happening.

74. 'It is a different blue I mean,' I say to Michelle. I try to explain about before and the blue

postcard with the blue stamp. She remembers then and she says she is sorry but she has no other blue postcards. She has some that are only red and some that are green and some that are yellow. Then she remembers that she had said that to me before and she laughs.

75. I do not really know if she remembered that she had said that before, but there was a look on her face that made me think that, a look in her eyes, which were blue after all.

76. 'He has been here every day for nearly two weeks,' the man at the next stall says. The man with the blue twenty-euro notes folded into a fist. He has leaned across to speak to Michelle and he nods at me so she knows who he means when he says '*he* has been here'. 'Not every day,' I say. Michelle dips her head and a lock of her hair falls across her cheek and she reaches up and with one finger of her hand she pushes the lock of hair back behind her ear.

77. Henri works late some nights. He sits in the back of the shop under a yellow light and he tacks the pieces of the suit together with wide stitches in a grey thread. The door to the shop is locked and everything is quiet and still, like a held breath, like the time between cutting and cut. Everything still, except for Henri's fingers, which are quick.

His face is lit up like gold or sunlight, though the skin under his eyes is pouched and blue.

78. Yves Klein continued to complete 'mono-chromes' – in pastel or in paint, blue and rose and yellow. Even as he was pursuing his black belt fourth dan he kept up his experiments in colour. It was as if he still did not know what he wanted to be when he grew up, even though he was already a man. Maybe this is also why he thought that one day time would have no past or future and would only have a present.

79. I do not know if Yves Klein's eyes were blue. Somehow it seems important to know this, but I have not read anywhere anything about the colour of his eyes.

80. There's a reproduction of a painting hanging on my wall in a plain wooden frame. It is by Dalí and it is like a page torn from a sketchbook; the page as though it has been soaked in rosehip tea and then dried. There are scribbles and scratches in brown ink in the corners, a brown church with a cupola and triangular pediments and steps leading to great doors. But at the bold centre of the page is a spilled splash of blue-grey, a wild ink splatter; underneath it some white. It is a swallow, though there is no red scarf for the bird. Maybe in Spain swallows do not wear the red.

81. Swallows are my favourite birds. I watch them from my window sometimes, following the perfectly drawn blue arcs they make in the sky, arcs that as soon as they are drawn are without line but not without shape or colour. Somehow I think Yves Klein would like that idea – shape in colour without edges and without lines.

82. 'Not every day,' I tell her. 'It was not every day. You must not think it was every day.' Michelle laughs again and she says he only teases, the man at the next stall. 'I was looking for another blue postcard,' I tell her and sometimes a thing said can be true and a lie both at the same time.

83. 'She does that thing with her hair that your mother used to do, exactly the same.' The voice of my father in my head used to have more shape and form and line to it. Now his voice is quieter than whisper so I almost do not hear the words but only feel them – the way some people feel blue or yellow or red. Yves Klein thought silence was green; he wrote this in a poem that explores the relationship between colour and emotion.

84. Henri has arranged for the man whose suit he is making to call again for a fitting. It is the usual way of things before the pieces of the suit are sewn together properly. The date and

the time of the fitting is entered into the ledger so Henri does not forget and so everything is ready. On arrival and after some pleasantries, the man is led through to the back room for a second time and he is shown into the space behind the curtain once again. He undresses and Henri hears the shush and shuck of cloth against the man's skin. When he steps from behind the curtain, Henri notices that he wears different-coloured socks, one grey and one blue. Henri smiles and begins helping the man into the suit that is not yet a suit.

85. Henri Matisse died on 3 November 1954. It was in that same year that Yves Klein, having returned from Japan, declared he was a painter. He published a catalogue of works in Madrid, the sort of publication that ordinarily accompanied an exhibition. There was no exhibition and there were no such works. He asked an artist friend, Claude Pascal, to write the introduction. What Pascal produced was three pages of horizontal lines arranged to look like printed paragraphs. I cannot decide if this act of publication was a white lie or a blue lie – from what came after it might be that it was a blue lie.

86. They are not simply blue, her eyes. They have something else adrift in the blue. There are shards of honeycomb there, too, small panned

golden flecks. Like the sky with the sun in it. Like pieces of a painting by Van Gogh, a self-portrait, torn pieces of his orange beard dropped on to the collar of his blue jacket.

87. You have to be close to see the orange in the blue.

88. On the colour wheel orange is directly opposite from blue.

89. This means that orange and blue are complementary colours.

90. Used next to each other complementary colours appear to be more intense than when used alone. Imagine then her eyes, both blue and orange. The orange seems to flash and spark and the blue is like flame.

91. 'Perhaps, when you are finished for the day and everything has been packed away and loaded into the back of your Peugeot 4DA van, circa 1952, the boxes of books and postcards and CDs, the fold-down tables and the awning, perhaps then we might go for a drink, if you can see past the years into an infinite present.' That is what I wanted to say. Instead I thanked her for her time and I said I would come again and maybe she would have another blue postcard then.

92. I wonder what colour regret is. I wonder if it is blue.

93. Henri says to the man in the mirror, the man with one blue sock on and one grey, that the suit will be completed by the end of the week. He makes a few marks in tailor's chalk to indicate further small adjustments he has to make, a dart here to pull the suit into the man's shape, a tuck to shorten one sleeve – for it is often the case that one arm is shorter than the other in a person. Henri takes some measurements again and adds them to the measurements he has written in the ledger. He wants to run his hand up the man's inside leg again, but it would not be proper to do so.

94. In 1955 Yves Klein produced a single colour matte-orange painting and submitted it to one of the salons in Paris. It was entitled *Expression de l'univers de la couleur mine orange* (*Expression of the Universe of the Orange Lead Colour*). It was at first accepted and then a few days later it was rejected. Perhaps without its complementary colour, blue, it lacked some spark.

95. Yves Klein asked his mother to intercede with the salon. They explained to her over the

phone that the painting, as it stood, was not really enough. They said they wanted a little something more than just orange. They offered to take the work if Yves Klein would only add a little something more to the painting, a mark maybe, a line or a point; or the touch of another colour, perhaps blue. Something more. Yves Klein refused.

96. 'One grey sock and one blue,' says Henri to himself. It is late again and he is working in the back of his shop, unpicking the tack stitches and sewing everything neat and straight, pressing in creases and giving the cloth shape with a hot iron.

97. Henri works on the jacket and trousers and waistcoat for three nights. He works till his eyes hurt and the stars are like ripples on water in the blue-blurred night sky.

98. Then at last, the finishing touch: Henri sews a twisted blue thread invisibly into the trousers somewhere, beneath the hem or the waistband, or hidden in a seam. It is Tekhelet and it is not for God but for luck. Henri wishes all his men to be lucky in their own way, for men, when they are lucky, credit what they are wearing with bringing them luck. And when the lucky suit wears thin as breath or wishing then they

return to the same lucky tailor for a second and a third lucky suit.

99. Michelle packs away her boxes of books and postcards and CDs. She collapses the tables and pushes the folded awning into a sack that smells of autumn leaves and burning and black earth. She loads everything into the back of the Peugeot 4DA van, circa 1952, looks briefly up at the Eiffel Tower trying to see where it touches the blue of the sky, and then she climbs into the van and drives off.

100. When the suit is complete, Henri hangs it on a wooden hanger. He is careful that the trousers hold their creases right and the waistcoat is buttoned and the jacket, too. He brushes the shoulders of the jacket with the flat of his hand as he will again when the man returns to try on his suit at the end of the week, and he says again under his breath, 'One grey sock and one blue.' He shakes his head, smiling to himself, and he hangs the finished suit on a rail in the back room.

II

Blue Lies

101. International Atomic Time (ATI) is a highly precise measurement of time. It is correct with a deviation of only one second in every 100 million years. But it seems to me, at my age, that time is much more elastic than ATI allows. I recall the blue lazy days of my youth and how five minutes was an interminably long time to wait for the postman to reach our house once I had seen him enter the street – and it was a longer time still on days when I was expecting a delivery of something. And now time slips so easily through my hands that a day passes in a blink sometimes and I do not know where it has gone.

102. My father used to say that patience was a blue virtue but he never said anything about impatience or what colour impatience might be. I do not think impatience is a vice.

103. Yves Klein was impatient to be someone and to measure up to something. The rejection of his painting *Expression de l'univers de la couleur mine orange* was a turning point for him. It gave him a name. He was talked about. He believed in striking while the iron was hot and he quickly arranged an exhibition of his work. Now that he had a deadline to meet, he worked at his paintings furiously, blue and red and yellow.

104. And this is when he had his first great success, though it did not at first look like a success and was not a blue ribbon event.

105. Michelle says she will look out for blue post-cards for me. I tell her they must be just blue and they must have a blue stamp on the reverse and the stamp must be franked 'Mai 1957'.

106. I notice that Michelle has a tattoo on the back of her right wrist. It is a small bird in flight and from the blue shape of its wings and its tail I would say it is a swallow.

107. Sailors used to get tattoos of swallows on their arms and their backs. It meant something then. It meant that they had sailed 5,000 miles. They got a fresh blue-inked swallow for every 5,000 miles they sailed.

108. I ask Michelle what the bird on the back of her wrist means. She says it is something to do with longing and gaps in time and being breathless. I look at her funny, as though I have not understood what she has said. Michelle tells me about the swallows of her childhood and how they built their spit-mud nests on the undersides of the eaves of her house. And she says she could see them from her bedroom

window, from her bed even, and she watched them coming and going all summer long, like blue darts. Then one day they were gone and summer ended long before she wanted it to.

109. Henri writes in his ledger when the suit is finished and when it has been collected. He puts the day and the date and how much he charged the customer. I should say that 'once' he wrote these things down but when I am talking about Henri I hope it is understood that we are in his time and not really in our time. If this was a film we might see Henri through a blue filter to show that his time is different.

110. On 15 October 1955, Yves Klein staged an exhibition of twenty of his monochrome paintings at the Club des Solitaires at 121 avenue de Villiers in Paris. Those that took the time to see the show responded with derision. One can imagine that the air was blue and loud was the sense of frustration at the waste of time it had been. But it was this strength of public response that attracted the attention of a critic called Pierre Restany who would go on to become the champion for Yves Klein's work.

111. It was around this time that Yves Klein's Aunt Rose, Tantine, sent him to get a good suit made. She forwarded money from Nice and the

card of a tailor in Paris that she understood to be good, maybe even the best. The card bore only the tailor's address, printed blue on white – though the white had yellowed a little and the corners of the card were dog-eared and rounded as though it had passed through many hands or pockets. So that Yves Klein thought maybe the tailor no longer lived or was now not as good as his aunt believed him to be.

112. There is a distance that comes between the paint when it is just pigment and how it appears on the canvas when the medium has dried. It is like something has been lost somewhere between the powdered blue and the finished painting – and not just the blue. This was a trouble to Yves Klein.

113. Not just with powdered blue, but rose and red and yellow pigments also. Indeed all colours can suffer this loss of intensity. It perhaps explains why artists seek to compensate for that something lost by putting complementary colours next to each other in an effort to replace the loss with a different intensity.

114. I tell Michelle I think her tattoo is pretty. I share with her my delight in swallows and the blue shapes they make in the air. I also tell her about the Dalí reproduction on my wall at

home, the one of the swallow. Maybe I am a little excited about what I say of the painting, a little breathless. She does not know the work. She says she would like to see it. Just like that.

115. I have held a swallow in my hands. It was dead. I found it in a field and scooped it up in my two hands, prayer-hands almost on that day. It looked as though it was sleeping, its blue wings like a straitjacket pinned to its side, the white of its breast like a new shirt out of the packet and the red of its scarf like fire. I blew on it, blew in its red face. There was a gap in time there and a breathlessness and not a little longing.

116. Henri has a bell fitted to the door of the shop so that no customer can enter or leave without announcing it. Yves Klein enters and the bell surprises him and delights him also. Henri steps out from the back of the shop. He is short and he wears a tape measure about his shoulders and his fingers are chalked blue. Yves Klein holds out the card his aunt sent him and the money. 'I need a good suit,' he says.

117. The reader of these stories will understand that there is truth and lies in the writing. Here is an example of what I mean: Yves Klein is both in Henri's shop at this point in the narrative (with

44

blue chalk on his inside leg) and at the same time was busy arranging his next exhibition at a gallery space on the rue d'Assomption owned by Colette Allendy. It is not that I am performing a thought experiment such as might be seen with Schrödinger's cat, but that time in this story is something fluid and shifting.

118. But let us for a moment apply the principle of Schrödinger's cat to Yves Klein, before his exhibition at Colette Allendy's place and before the intervention of the critic Pierre Restany. At this point in time Yves Klein is both someone and no one. Both possibilities are held in Yves Klein at this moment so both are real even though they are also contradictory. The future is a blue mist where both exist and only time will pull back the curtain to make the big reveal.

119. Henri writes Yves Klein's name on a fresh page in the ledger, a small blue hurrah in the upward kick of his pen at the end of the 'n' in Yves Klein's name. He writes down the young man's measurements underneath and the name of the suit cloth the man has chosen. He sets a date for a fitting and he nods and bids Yves Klein a good day.

120. It is not so simple to produce monochrome canvases as you would think. Yves Klein was no child splashing on colour any which way.

He applied himself to his work with an intensity of thought and a rigour of process that might be seen in any creative person in the act of creating. He was troubled by the gap between what was in his pigment box and what ended up on his canvas. He consulted with chemical engineers engaged with the production of fixatives and had a special compound made that allowed the blue to remain blue, the red to remain red and the yellow to remain yellow.

121. It was 'The Minute of Truth', which coincidentally was the title of an essay written by Pierre Restany championing Yves Klein's new art, arguing that it was art that stood outside time and offered the promise of quiet in a busy industrial world. Yves Klein's art, he said, provided the opportunity for total contemplation in the spectator. A sort of blue truth as opposed to a blue lie.

122. Michelle looks somehow smaller when she is not behind her stall below the Eiffel Tower. I offer her a seat and a drink. I have some wine in for the occasion, for that is what I think of her visit to my apartment – an occasion. I have tidied up and arranged my collection of blue things on the windowsill so that they might catch her eye. And the postcard trapped between two pieces of Perspex is propped up on the mantelpiece showing the blue side.

123. 'Blue,' she says when she sees the glass of wine I set before her. The wine is a white wine, a bottle of Crémant. It has a sparkle to it. The glass is blue and from Venice. It was one of a set of six but it is the last one left. My father says I should have poured the wine into the willow pattern bowl made in Stoke-on-Trent, England; it was something my father wished for.

124. I show Michelle the Dalí reproduction of the blue ink-splash swallow and she gasps and holds one hand over her mouth as though she is holding back words, holding her breath, holding the moment on her tongue.

125. 'It is my new favourite painting,' she says when she has found her words and she sucks in air and blows it out again from her cheeks. I notice that she is still wearing her name badge as if her name is something I might forget. And the sleeve of her sweater is pushed up to her elbow so I can see her very own blue swallow, which I want to say is *my* new favourite painting.

126. Maybe I said that thing about time in this novel being fluid because it is something I wish it was. I am old. Foolishly old. As old as my father was when he breathed his last breath. And Michelle is new and the world that she

sees is pure blue and pure red and pure yellow. It is all the colours of the rainbow and all the colours I cannot see but wish I could.

127. Henri waits for the bell above the door to stop ringing. Then he breathes, sucks and blows air as though he is a swimmer who surfaces now from a deep dive. He holds his hands to his face and inhales the smell of Yves Klein that clings to his fingers along with the blue chalk. He says a prayer then, and it is the first that he has spoken for many years. Maybe it is to God and maybe it is not – for prayers can be things given up to the infinite blue nothing. And what Henri prays for is that time might collapse then and there, or concertina, so that the day of Yves Klein's fitting could be present and pressing.

128. Now he was someone – Yves Klein – and his name was something that could be heard over dinner in fine restaurants or spoken in whispers in art classrooms. Not yet a great blue shout, but it was a start.

129. He was invited to join the Order of St Sebastian. The ceremony of his induction into the order is recorded in a black and white photograph. His chosen coat of arms was a blue monochrome with the handwritten motto: 'For Colour! Against line and drawing.'

130. At the same time as his star was rising in the blue and infinite sky, his mother and father's marriage collapsed (you see how not just in a novel but in real life time can contain many events all happening to the one person and all at the same time, for when a marriage collapses it collapses on the children as much as on the parents even when the child is twenty-eight years old and must be considered a man).

131. St Sebastian was an early Christian martyr. On the Roman emperor Diocletian's orders and as part of the emperor's persecution of Christians, Sebastian was tied to a tree and shot through with arrows. However, this did not kill him. He was rescued by St Irene and nursed back to health. His eyes I think were blue.

132. I have a blue seashell on my windowsill, beside the blue-grey stone and the blue church glass. A blue fountain pen is there, too, a Bayard Excelsior fountain pen. Perhaps it is the same pen that Henri has in his inside jacket pocket and which he uses to record the names and measurements of the men who visit his shop that used to be on the Street of Tailors and now is surrounded by cafés and bars and a shop that sells only gloves.

133. 'Everything blue,' Michelle says.

134. What colour are thoughts, I wonder, and dreams? I used to think I dreamed in colour, now I am not so sure. But they are not black and white either, not like pictures in old books or like old TV. They have an inkiness to them that makes me think they might be blue, the blue of ink that in the bottle looks as though it is black.

135. 'You may come and see Dalí's swallow any time you like,' I tell her. Then it is a little awkward, as though I have suggested something indecent, something blue. She finishes her wine, drains it in a single draught. I expect her to go then but she asks if there is any more wine in the bottle.

136. Henri closes up the shop. He pulls to the wooden shutters on the window and locks them – for he remembers a long-ago night when glass was something to be broken. He slips the key into his waistcoat pocket. Then he walks, following where his feet take him, which is down to the river and past the lit-up ship that is Notre-Dame. He bends to pick up stones big as fists and he puts them in his pockets – all his pockets. Above him there might be stars in the sky but when he looks the whole of heaven swirls and swings, like the application of blue

paint in Van Gogh's *Starry Night*, and though he does not know it there are salted tears on his cheeks and he is praying again.

137. Sometimes, even for the old, time is something slow and creeping. There is a darkness in the room and I do not know how it suddenly came there, a street-light darkness which is soft and blue and not really dark at all. Michelle has fallen asleep in the chair, her legs pulled up beneath her. I do not know what to do then, do not know if I should wake her, do not dare to. I say her name, but I say it only so loud as it might not disturb her sleep. I use my coat to cover her and retreat to the bedroom, leaving her blue and sleeping and like something I only dreamed.

138. In November 1956 Yves Klein had enough money he could rent a studio at 9 rue Campagne-Première in the centre of the artists' quarter at Montparnasse. He wanted another exhibition and he wanted it as quickly as possible so he visited Iris Clert who owned a new gallery. He presented her with an orange monochrome painting for her consideration. He left it with her for a week to see what effect it might have on her. Sometimes she stared at the work, stared and stared, and when she looked away the whole world was strangely blue.

139. Iris Clert displayed Yves Klein's orange monochrome painting in the window of her small gallery and looked to see if the people passing saw the world blue afterwards. They shook their fists at the painting and spat on the pavement and laughed cruelly. Iris Clert saw that the painting had some power even if she was not sure what that power was exactly.

140. Then Yves Klein was invited to exhibit in Milan. This is sometimes called the start of his *époque bleue*, his blue period. There were reasons for his switch to blue monochrome works. In his earlier exhibitions he saw how observers were distracted by the relationships between the colours, and this was not what Yves Klein was aiming for. He wanted the viewer to experience a greater contemplation of each individual work.

141. For Yves Klein blue was without dimension.

142. Blue was suggestive.

143. Blue suggested the sea and the sky.

144. When I wake she is gone. There is a held quiet in the apartment. It feels like an absence of more than sound. It feels like a blue dream, the one where I am looking in a hundred rooms

and not ever finding what it is I am looking for and not ever knowing either.

145. That is a lie. They come a lot easier once the first has been told. I heard her get up from the chair and look around and find her bearings. I heard her fold the coat she had slept under – my coat – and I heard her lay it down on the chair. She looked at Dalí's blue ink swallow one last time, was still and breathless in front of it. Then she picked up her shoes and crept from the room. I heard her shut the front door, careful not to make a noise above the click of the Yale lock. Then it was that I heard the absence of sound.

146. Henri is a little late to his shop the next day. There are no appointments in his book, only orders that have to be met. He had cut out the cloth for Yves Klein's suit the night before and then he had taken the idea of that suit home with him. There were small flourishes he could add to the suit that he would not charge for, just as he did not charge for the blue thread he sewed into the seams. He wanted to do this for Yves Klein. He looks in the mirror in the back room and imagines the young man – who was in fact no younger or older than Henri – standing tall beside him. He imagines slipping his hand into the hand of the artist and holding fast.

147. I have tried to find out how tall Yves Klein was so that I could imagine him standing next to Henri in the mirror, but there is no information on this to be found. I do not know if he wore blue socks or grey, or one of each; or if he kept his shoes on when he stepped out from behind the curtain in Henri's back room; or if he shook a little when Henri ran his tape measure up his inside leg.

148. Henri does not open the wooden shutters on his shop window that day. I do not think anyone notices. He locks the door behind him once he has entered the shop and he goes straight through to the back room where the shape of Yves Klein is cut into pieces on the table. Henri does not remove his coat but picks up the blue tailor's chalk and begins to make quick small adjustments to the cloth, adjustments that will make the suit worth more than the money Yves Klein's Aunt has sent.

149. 'Is that it? She just goes and you let her go?' It is the voice of my father again – or, if not his voice, his thoughts in my head. I am standing in front of the Dalí swallow and I am wearing my coat, the one Michelle had slept under. It smells a little of her. Looking at the reproduction of Dalí's painting I do not today see blue but

something less than blue. I think that is what growing old must be.

150. In early January 1957 Yves Klein exhibited under the title: *Proposte monocrome: epoca blu* (*Monochrome Propositions: Blue Epoch*). The exhibition was housed at the Galleria Apollinaire on the via Brera in Milan.

151. All the canvases were blue, a uniform blue. He again used the special fixative solution developed in 1956 by Edouard Adam and the company Rhône-Poulenc. He combined this with a particular shade of ultramarine marketed as number 1311.

152. There are secret instructions on how to combine the constituent components that go together to make Yves Klein's special blue. Everything has to be weighed and measured and the conditions under which the ingredients must be combined are strict. The threat of danger hangs over the process if the mixture is ever heated.

153. In 1957 – the year I was born – Yves Klein arrived at a final recipe for the blue that he patented as International Klein Blue (IKB). It is perhaps what remains of Yves Klein today in the public consciousness.

154. The audacity, to have a colour carry your name!
Like putting your signature across the blue sky.

155. Michelle is there at the foot of the Eiffel Tower.
That is what I imagine. The man at the next
stall looks her up and down and he nods to
himself and smiles. She is wearing the same
dress as the day before. The dress is creased, her
hair is tangled and she looks a little crumpled
– and she is smiling and singing to herself and
moving from the back of the Peugeot 4DA van,
circa 1952, to the fold-down tables. Well, it
looks to the man at the next stall as though
Michelle might be dancing.

156. 'It's not what you think,' Michelle says to
the man at the next stall. He holds his hands
up empty as if he is not thinking anything at
all. 'Flowers have meaning,' he says and he
taps one finger against the side of his nose.
'The blue cornflower on your dress signifies
an abundance of good fortune.' He holds his
hands up empty again. That is all he says and
he shakes his head and laughs.

157. I do not know why it was the man at the next
stall who noticed the blue cornflowers printed
on to her dress. I do not know why I did not see
this before when she was sleeping curled up in
the armchair in my apartment.

158. Blue is a painted vault.

159. Blue is a flame.

160. Blue is obscurity become visible, a space of indeterminate reverie.

161. Henri pins the interface to the wool and tacks the pieces of the jacket together – not quick stitches this time, but slow and lingering – and he dresses the shop mannequin to look like Yves Klein. Then he stands in front of the mirror in the back room, stands next to the dummy Yves Klein and he holds the cuff of one sleeve, in the absence of a hand. He does not notice that he leaves a blue smeared fingerprint of tailor's chalk pressed on to the cloth.

162. A man dressed smart as paint – which is something my father used to say – entered the Galleria Apollinaire on the via Brera in Milan. He did not know what to expect except that he'd overheard someone talking about the Frenchman and his eleven blue canvases. He stood quite still before the first canvas and he was quite breathless.

163. He lost himself in the blue as though he'd stepped into the painting he was standing

before. They were all the same, those eleven blue canvases and yet they were also all of them different. He did not understand how that was, how that could be.

164. He returned to the Galleria Apollinaire over the next three days and he stood in front of a different blue canvas each time.

165. An important Italian writer, Dino Buzzati, penned an article for the *Corriere d'Informazione*. Its title was 'Blu, Blu, Blu'. With its talk of madmen and revolutionaries and fanatics of the extreme avant-garde it brought people to the exhibition in great numbers.

166. It was a different experience each time. Maybe it was something holy on that first day, like touching the blue cloth of the Madonna in Raffaello Sanzio's painting of *The Marriage of the Virgin* (1504) at the Pinacoteca di Brera in Milan.

167. And on the second day, in front of the seventh blue canvas, it was something else – first it was nothing, and then it was a deep nothing and then it was only a blue depth. They are not his thoughts exactly, but something he read in Gaston Bachelard's *La poétique de l'espace* (*The Poetics of Space*).

168. And on the third day it was a blue dream. A dream that was without borders and was only infinite.

169. On that third day the man, dressed as smart as paint, attracted the attention of the owner of the gallery. The owner stepped from behind his desk and asked if he could be of any assistance. The smartly dressed man nodded and he said he would like to purchase the blue painting he was at that moment lost in.

170. The smartly dressed man walked out of the gallery with the painting wrapped in blue cloth under his arm. His name was Italo Magliano and once he was a tailor – no less and no other than the tailor to Benito Mussolini.

171. I want to give Michelle Dalí's blue swallow picture but I do not know what this will mean if I do. My father shakes his head, just as the man at the next stall to Michelle's shakes his head. They know.

172. I have a blue cotton shirt. Once it was the colour of night but it has been washed so many times it is now the colour of day. I tear the shirt into pieces and use one of the pieces to wrap the picture in.

173. I rehearse presenting the picture to Michelle without leaving the room of my apartment. I imagine her there, in her blue flower-print dress and she takes the painting and unfolds the blue cloth to discover Dalí's swallow. She breathes on to its feathers and it takes flight and swoops and dips in the air of my front room. It is just a dream, except that I have the painting wrapped in a piece of my blue shirt and I do so want to give it to Michelle.

174. The exhibition in Milan ran from 2 January to 12 January. The eleven paintings, all a monochrome blue with rounded corners and all of them as near the same size as can be, were hung with space between the pictures and the wall, so that they projected into the space where the viewer stood. Yves Klein hung them deliberately at different heights to the viewer and so the experience of each work was different from the rest.

175. There was one red monochrome, but it was not part of *l'époque bleue* exhibition. It was presented to the gallery owner, Guido Le Noci, and it was hung in his private office. The red monochrome was subsequently sold to an important Milanese art collector called Giuseppe Panza di Biumo. He took the painting

home and stared at it for a day before returning the work to the Galleria Apollinaire having changed his mind.

176. Henri stands next to the trouserless dummy Yves Klein, holding on to the sleeve of its jacket, until blue night creeps into the room and he can no longer see himself or the dummy Yves Klein reflected in the glass of the mirror. He sighs and lets go of the jacket sleeve.

177. Yves Klein later alleged that the blue paintings in his exhibition, though all of the same size and the same colour with little to differentiate between them, had been priced differently.

178. On his return to Paris Yves Klein began the process of fanning the blue flames of his success. These might be called white lies or they might be blue.

179. They might also be called fictions, for what else is fiction but a manufactured lie even when it holds truth? Yves Klein bragged that he had sold each of his eleven blue canvases to the Italians.

180. It is of no matter that the truth is he sold only three of his *l'époque bleue* works.

181. He also claimed that the public saw each of his blue paintings as a distinct work, different from one another, each with a unique essence and each with its own atmosphere.

182. On his return to Paris he presents himself to the tailor his aunt had recommended. He is there for his fitting as arranged and as recorded in the ledger that Henri keeps. Henri is, as might be expected, pleased to see the young man. He thinks there is something different about him. Yves Klein stands a little straighter perhaps or he smiles more or there is a light in him, blue like gaslight.

183. Yves Klein does not stop for breath but talks through the entire hour of the fitting. He tells Henri of his Milan exhibition and of how he had conquered the Italians. He boasts that he'd sold all eleven of his blue paintings and if he'd had a hundred more paintings and all of them blue they would have sold, too.

184. Henri stands in front of the mirror next to Yves Klein in his tacked and pinned-together new suit. 'You have to imagine it finished and pressed sharp as knives and not a loose thread anywhere to be seen.' Henri holds on to the sleeve of the jacket and his blue dream is briefly real.

185. Sometimes for the young time is fleeting and quickly lost. It skips away without ever being noticed that it is going. Michelle thinks the man at the next stall must be packing up early. She looks down at her watch to check the time, but there is no watch. She checks her other wrist, the one with the blue swallow tattoo, but her watch is missing from there also.

186. Then she asks the man at the next stall why he is finishing so early. When she discovers it is not early but late she begins packing up, too. 'I do not know where the time has gone today,' she calls over to the man at the next stall. 'Check the pocket of your blue dress,' he calls back to her.

187. In the pocket of Michelle's blue dress is a blue stone, except that the stone is dry and so it looks grey. It is small enough it could fit in her mouth but she does not know this yet. It means something, but she does not know what.

188. The bell above the door of Henri's shop rings and the door closes and Yves Klein is not real any more and not standing beside Henri in the mirror in the back room. The sound of the bell, which earlier had been so musical and dancing, is now church-like and dull; it is the same bell

but it is Henri's experience of it that is different. He thinks this was something Yves Klein had said to him about the experience of people in front of his blue paintings, all of them the same but the experience of each different.

189. Henri enters into the ledger the date and time for Yves Klein's next visit, the date when the suit must be finished and the lucky blue thread sewn into the hem of his trousers or the waistband. He caps the blue Bayard Excelsior fountain pen and slips it back into his jacket inside pocket.

190. The blue thread must be twisted. Henri has one ready. He wraps it loosely round his finger again and again until he is wearing a ring of blue. It means something but Henri dare not say what.

191. Once she is home, Michelle kicks off her shoes and takes the stone out of her pocket. She undresses, shedding her clothes on to the floor of the bathroom and she steps into the shower still holding the stone. The water is cold and she snatches for breath. When she looks again at the stone in her hand it is wet and blue.

192. In fiction the writer can hold things back from the reader. It is understood. Though when he

then reveals those things they can seem like magic, like the man at the bottom of the steps at *Le Passage de la Sorcière* in Montmartre with his silver egg cups and his wooden ball the size of a pea and the ball is found under the cup that you least expect it to be under. The blue stone that Michelle holds in her hand under the shower is my stone, as will have been guessed, but how it came to be in her pocket is not the mystery that it might appear. I dropped it into her pocket as she slept and before I pulled my coat as a blanket over her.

193. How the man at the next stall knew about the stone, well that was an error that an editor would take his blue pencil to. It doesn't make sense that the man at the next stall would know this. It would be enough that Michelle discovered the stone in her pocket by herself.

194. As for Michelle's watch, I find it at the end of the day, when I am clearing up the remaining torn scraps of my blue cotton shirt. I know it immediately and I resolve to return it the next day. My father nods. 'Aha!' he exclaims, but I do not hear the exclamation and only know it as a thought.

195. Henri locks the door to his shop and slips the key into his waistcoat pocket. He feels the

blue thread ring still about his finger, rubs it against the ball of his thumb – for luck or for something else.

196. And Yves Klein believed what he told his friends: 'They came in their thousands. So many that they had to be turned away. They were queuing round the block and the manager of the gallery had to arrange for water to be taken out to them in blue cups.'

197. By this time everything was blue for Yves Klein.

198. 'And what has been done in Milan can be done again here in Paris and who knows but after that the whole world could be painted blue.'

199. When the stone on Michelle's windowsill dries to a dull grey, she picks it up and kisses it and licks it till it is blue once more. But it does not take long for it to dry again.

200. Before she gets into her bed, she fills a glass with water and drops the stone into the glass so it will still be blue when she wakes in the morning.

III

Stones in Pockets

201. Yves Klein returns to Henri's shop on the morning of 20 January 1957. Henri hears the bell above the door ring and can scarcely contain his pleasure. He invites Yves Klein into the back of the shop again and presents him with his new suit. 'It would be best for you to try it on to see how it looks.' Yves Klein slips behind the curtain to undress. The jacket and the trousers are made from a dark blue cloth; the waistcoat is a bright and burning red.

202. Like a swallow he looks when he is dressed. And as he was so fond of waving his arms in the air when he spoke he looks like a swallow in flight. He is delighted with his new suit. He shakes Henri's hand again and again. 'So blue and so red,' he says. 'I shall purchase a gold watch and chain and then it will be everything I want in a suit.'

203. The ringing of the bell above the door of Henri's shop catches the attention of Yves Klein just as he is about to step out into the street again. He holds the door, his head canted to one side in a pantomime of listening. He hears the one blue note of the bell thinning into nothing.

204. 'I found it under one of the cushions of my armchair. It is yours, I think.' It sounds a little formal said like that. I catch my father's face in the mirror. I can see he thinks so, too. His blue eyes

68

flash and his yellow teeth show when he laughs. 'Just give the watch to her. Nothing more than that. It will be enough.' That's what my father thinks and maybe what he says, too, for in the mirror I see his lips make the shapes of the words.

205. 'You left this. You did not mean to, I think.' It makes no sense to rehearse the words we are going to say for we cannot in our rehearsal anticipate all things. Maybe when I approach her stall at the foot of the Eiffel Tower I will be interrupted in my speech by the barking of a white dog in a blue collar.

206. Maybe an old woman with blue hair will reach in front of me to pick up one of Michelle's books, thinking that if she does not do this I might purchase it ahead of her.

207. Maybe something will catch Michelle's eye – a blue falling swallow perhaps, for I have seen swallows flying under the arched feet of the Eiffel Tower and I know how fond she is of swallows – and then I will be speaking to the back of her head. Or the words will come out of my mouth stumbling and Michelle will have to ask me to say them again. Or there will be a noise to compete with my words and so they will be something hidden or lost.

208. Later in the afternoon, Yves Klein wore his blue suit and red waistcoat to a fete held to celebrate St Sebastian's feast day. Heads turned and that is exactly what he wanted.

209. St Sebastian is the patron saint of archers and pin-makers. There was much drumming at the fete to celebrate the saint's feast day that Yves Klein attended in Paris. As well as a gold watch and chain, he had purchased a blue handkerchief, which he wore foppishly protruding from his breast pocket.

210. Henri closes the shop early. If I seem to be always saying that he closes his shop it is only because this is something he does every day. I omit to say that he sweeps the floor of his shop once a week and dusts the shelves and washes the front window at some time in the month or at a time when the sky no longer looks so blue through the glass. This day, 20 January, the feast day of St Sebastian, Henri closes the shop early and walks with some apparent purpose down to the river to look for stones.

211. He crosses to the middle of the Pont Neuf and climbs over the stone lip to stand on the ledge. He looks down into the water. Maybe to Henri it looks blue with possibility. He is a little unsteady and reaches back to stop himself from

falling. The pockets of his coat click with the stones that he carries. As do his jacket pockets and there are bulges in his trouser pockets, too.

212. There are some who have thrown themselves into the Seine from the ledge of the Pont Neuf. It happens sometimes: lovers that have had their hearts broken beyond repair; men who have lost fortunes; women who should be mothers and briefly were and are not mothers any more. Henri twists a strand of blue thread through his fingers.

213. A gendarme approaches Henri and asks if he would please climb back over the stone lip, which Henri manages only with a display of effort due to the stones he is carrying. The gendarme asks Henri for his name and he writes it down in a blue notebook that he keeps in the breast pocket of his blue shirt. Henri does as he is asked and the gendarme claps him on the back and sends him on his way.

214. In May 1957 Yves Klein featured in two Paris exhibitions. One at the Galerie Iris Clert on the Left Bank of the Seine and the other at the Galerie Colette Allendy on the Right Bank. This was a rerun of his *Proposte Monocrome* exhibition in Milan with more of his blue paintings.

215. To advertise these exhibitions Yves Klein produced a monochrome blue postcard, the same IKB blue of his paintings.

216. He also produced a blue perforated stamp for the reverse of the postcards and bribed an official at the French post office to accept the stamps as legitimate postage.

217. The blue postcards with their blue stamps became artworks in themselves and were soon much prized among collectors.

218. Michelle is there at her stall at the bottom of the Eiffel Tower. If I seem to repeat this in the same way that I repeat that Henri opens and closes his shop it is only because Michelle is so often there at the foot of the Eiffel Tower. She is not wearing blue today. Nor is she wearing rose or gold or anything that resembles these colours. Today she is dressed all in white. She sees me before I reach her stall and she waves.

219. You see, that is not something I expected and so not something that I factored in when I was practising what I would say to her at the handing over of her watch, not the white of her dress or her waving. And so I do as my dead father instructed me: I simply hold out the watch for her to take with no words. Michelle laughs and she thanks

me and does not ask after any explanation. She also does not give back the blue stone that she must by now have found in her dress pocket.

220. Henri does not open his shop again for a month. When this is noticed by others in the street they say at first that he must be away on holiday, though Henri has never taken a holiday before. It is something that has become fashionable, they say, and so they think he is enjoying the blue of sea and sky somewhere in the south – maybe in Nice.

221. When Henri does not return after two weeks, the talk then is that he was ill and some dare to say that he died, even going so far as to invent the manner in which he died. One woman leaves a bouquet of blue flowers at the door of Henri's shop. There is no message attached and by the time Henri does return to his shop the flowers are no longer blue and have been trampled into the pavement.

222. Pierre Restany, Yves Klein's critic champion, provided a handwritten text for the reverse of his blue postcards.

223. The text is brief and yet at the same time overblown, trumpeting the purity of the blue pigment that would be on show in the two concurrent exhibitions and heralding in the era of blue.

224. The addresses of the two galleries are also printed on the reverse of the blue postcards.

225. The blue postcards were sent out as invitations to Yves Klein's exhibitions.

226. Henri received his blue postcard invitation but chose not to attend the exhibition. He walked by the window of Iris Clert's gallery one evening. It was the smaller of the two exhibition spaces. On display he saw several of Yves Klein's blue monochromes and a sculpture using natural sponges soaked in an ultramarine pigment.

227. What Henri did not witness, for he did not enter Iris Clert's gallery, was that the exhibition had an accompanying soundtrack – Yves Klein's one-note musical composition entitled *Monotone Symphony*. The piece was recorded by a classical pianist of some repute. If Henri had entered the gallery he would have heard a sound not unlike the blue tone of the ringing bell above his shop door. And just maybe hearing it would have meant something to Henri.

228. As well as the postcards with their blue stamps franked by the French post office (for a fee), Yves Klein arranged for the release of 1,001 blue helium-filled balloons to advertise the opening of the exhibition at Galerie Iris Clert.

229. 'Tell me about the postcards and why they must be blue.'

230. I am surprised it has not come up till now, this question from Michelle about the postcards. 'Have you heard of International Klein Blue?' I ask her.

231. She hasn't, but then why would she? It is more than fifty years later and there are no blue balloons hanging in the air above Paris today, only red ones and not so many as 1,001.

232. She laughs when I tell her about the exhibition of blue paintings. They are still laughing at Yves Klein fifty years later.

233. Not just paintings but sculptures, too, and tapestries, all of them blue. With one he used thin wooden extensions that hung from the ceiling of the Galerie Colette Allendy. The pieces were painted blue and bore the title *Blue Rain*.

234. And on the floor blue granules of Pure Pigment, like sand raked into coiling patterns – like Van Gogh's *Starry Night* laid on the floor and everyone walking over the blue sky.

235. For the opening of the exhibition at Galerie Colette Allendy on 14 May 1957 – which

you may recall is my birth date – Yves Klein provided a further spectacle. He attached sixteen Bengal Flares to a blue monochrome painting placed on an easel and lit them all simultaneously. They burned for a minute.

236. I do not tell Michelle that my birthday is 14 May 1957. I just tell her about the blue flames and the blue rain and everything blue.

237. Henri reads about Yves Klein in the newspapers. There are pictures, too. He uses his tailor's scissors to cut out those pictures – holding his breath from the start of the cut to the end – and he pins the pictures up on the wall behind the mirror in the back room of his shop. They are out of the light there and so they do not yellow quickly. He attaches a piece of the blue cloth that he used to make Yves Klein's suit, and a piece of the red of his waistcoat and a twist of blue thread that he has secretly sewn into the pockets of his trousers so that Yves Klein might always be touching Tekhelet for luck.

238. 'What is it with all things blue?' Michelle asks.

239. It is a good question. One that has troubled researchers for decades. However, one thing is certain, and established beyond all reasonable doubt: the world's favourite colour is blue, some shade of blue at least.

240. When it comes to explaining *why* blue is so much loved, then the research is a little woolly. It maybe has something to do with associations that are attached to blue, which are mostly positive.

241. Blue is associated with sky and sea or clean water.

242. And eyes and ink and jeans can all be blue.

243. You see how woolly it becomes and how the question of why blue is the world's favourite colour quickly loses its meaning?

244. 'It is my favourite colour, too,' Michelle concedes. 'But I don't collect all things blue or surround myself with only blue.'

245. I shrug and hold my hands up empty. (Yes, I know I have used that gesture before with the man at the next stall, but you easily understand what it says and so it is a sort of shorthand for my not knowing or not being able to say). 'Blue is all around us anyway,' I tell Michelle.

246. Then there's a swallow that catches our attention, flying in perfect curves under the metal arched feet of the Eiffel Tower – I knew there would be a swallow there at some time

and I knew it would distract me from what I was saying; I did not know it would distract Michelle from her question about blue.

247. 'I should like to make a gift of the Dalí picture to you.'
'Really? Why?'
'I don't know. No reason.'
'Huh.'
'My father thinks there's a reason.'
'Your father?'
'My dead father.'
'I'm sorry.'
'No, it was a long time ago.'
'I don't understand.'
'He thinks it's because you do this thing with your hair.'
'Thing?'
'Yes, with your finger, and you tuck your hair behind one ear.'
'Don't all girls do that?'
'Not all. My mother used to do it – at least my father said she did.'
'Back to your father.'
'I see him sometimes, a blue-mist vision of him.'

248. It's not how I would have said it if I'd had time to practise it. My father wouldn't have let me say it like that. He'd have laughed and made it all simple. 'Just give her the picture,' he would

have said. 'Wrapped in the blue shirt-cloth. She will get what it means.'

249. The woman who left the blue flowers outside Henri's shop laughs when she sees him walking past her window. Well, at first she starts as though she has seen a ghost, which of course he could well have been. Then she recovers herself and she laughs.

250. She calls in at his shop the next morning and she says she is glad to see him up and about and looking so well. 'I had thought you must be dead,' she says. 'Then I saw you yesterday, walking past my window and you're not dead. A little smaller perhaps, and quieter, quiet as blue shadows. I thought I was seeing a ghost. Everyone was saying you must be dead, you see, so I left flowers at the door of your shop. And here you are not dead.'

251. Of course, time in this narrative is looped and it doubles back on itself and threads – blue threads – that are dropped sometimes stay dropped (which will be called bad writing) and sometimes they will be picked up again (and that may well be called bad writing also).

252. Yves Klein had one more trick up his sleeve that May in 1957 – yes, I know calling it a 'trick' is something more akin to the blue-stone-toothed

man at the foot of the steps at *Le Passage de la Sorcière* in Montmartre with his silver eggcups and his disappearing wooden ball. Yves Klein had a separate exhibit upstairs on the second floor of the Galerie Colette Allendy. This was not open to the general public but was shown only to a select few invited guests.

253. Yves Klein called this hidden work *Surfaces and Blocks of Invisible Pictorial Sensibility*. Nothing blue here. Indeed, nothing at all. The whole space had been painted white and left totally empty.

254. Remember the man sitting at the bottom of the steps at *Le Passage de la Sorcière* in Montmartre and how he said I was to lift the egg cup I had chosen and to do it with a flourish to make something of the big reveal and when I did the wooden ball was not there and was not anywhere? Remember that he laughed and scooped up my money and put it in his pocket? When I think of Yves Klein and his room that is an absence of blue and an absence of all colour and all things, then I think of that man at the bottom of the steps at *Le Passage de la Sorcière* in Montmartre.

255. 'You and I are the only ones who remember that this was a whole street of tailors once. There is a responsibility in us, a responsibility

to them. We must keep going.' The woman of the blue flowers makes a point of dropping into Henri's shop once a day. Maybe she has seen something in the man. Maybe she is aware of the pictures pinned to the wall behind the mirror in the back room. Maybe she has a need that is as great as Henri's and that is why she keeps on calling.

256. 'I remember your grandfather. I can picture him sitting in a wooden armchair outside the front of the shop. Wrapped in a prayer shawl some days, tipping his hat at all the other tailors in the street. They were a community and if one of the tailors ran out of white thread then his neighbour would provide him with a reel from his own shelf. Or if one was short of blue buttons then he might trade with another, swapping buttons for bread.'

257. 'He sewed my wedding dress. And he did not charge me one franc for the work. My mother said she'd never seen the like for the dress was white and I do not think girls with no money married in white then. It was only after the wedding that I found the twisted blue thread that your grandfather had stitched into the seam. I think he did that so I would be nearer to God – his God.'

258. 'I should like to make a gift of the Dalí picture to you.'

(There, I am replaying it and playing it differently from how it was.)

'Really? Why?'

'Because I can see how much you love it. As much as I love it and why wouldn't a person want to share that? And when you stop loving it – if ever you do – then you must promise me you will pass it on as I am passing it to you.'

(You see that I have inserted 'love' into the conversation and have not mentioned blue.)

259. Yves Klein exhibited his blue monochromes in Düsseldorf after Paris and then in London after Düsseldorf. He was soon able to declare himself as famous as Picasso and of course he did.

260. In July 1957 Yves Klein met Rotraut Uecker on a trip to Nice. Maybe he wore his blue suit with his red waistcoat and gold watch and chain. Certainly, his Aunt Rose, Tantine, would have wanted to see what her money had bought. Rotraut Uecker was extraordinarily beautiful and Yves Klein was lit up with the success he had had. They spent a month together in Nice, day and night inseparable.

261. Then he returned to Paris intent on the further pursuit of fame. His next project was an

extension of *Surfaces and Blocks of Invisible Pictorial Sensibility*. He exhibited again at the Galerie Iris Clert in April 1958. The show was called *The Void*. Like the small private second-floor exhibit of the previous year that was seen only by Yves Klein's intimate circle, there was almost nothing of blue in *The Void*.

262. 'Tekhelet,' Henri says. Then he goes on to explain to the woman who had left blue flowers at his door all about Tekhelet and what it says in his book and about the special dye that is excreted by the sea snail *Murex trunculus* and how this is done every seven years, though the book says seventy years, which is commonly thought to be an error.

263. Henri shows her his prayer shawl and the white tassels that he calls 'tzitzit' and the blue Tekhelet threads in the four corner tassels. He says he no longer prays and that is because of what had happened to his grandfather and to his father. He does not need to say anything more.

264. 'And what would bring you back to God, I wonder?' says the woman of the blue flowers. She takes Henri's hand in hers and pats it like it is a pet. 'We have not time enough to be angry at the end. We have to let some things go.'

265. I help her at the end of the day. I help her pack away her boxes of postcards and books and CDs, everything carried into the back of the Peugeot 4DA van, circa 1952, the van that was once blue and now is no colour at all except that it is near to grey. I fold down the tables and they are put into the van, too. Then I climb in the front beside Michelle.

266. I could of course invent a love story at this point. I do not know how that would be received. I am old and Michelle is young and the difference is something that everyone can see. And the old are somehow not allowed to love, not like the young at least. Michelle takes my hand in hers and she says I am sweet and she confesses that she has stolen something that belongs to me and she says it is the stone from my windowsill. She does not tell me about licking the stone and kissing it and taking it with her into the shower until it is blue. But somehow I know.

267. I do not think a stone can be said to belong to a person. I tell her about the stone and how I picked it up out of a river and it was blue until it dried and then it was only blue in possibility. I tell her that I like that most especially, that blue can be something that adheres in a thing

and at the same time can be something hidden. I do not tell her that I think love is something the same.

268. 'Do you believe in angels, Henri?' He does not know what she means with her question. She presents him with a feather that he thinks at first is white – like her wedding dress must have been – and then he looks a little closer and there is blue in the feather, too.

269. 'The wings of angels are sometimes shown as white and taller than the tallest man and folded like heavy cloaks at their backs. It was not always so. There is a painting I have seen but I do not now recall the name of the artist or the title of the work, but the angels I do remember and their wings are all colours – red and green and blue and orange.'

270. 'I do not know if there are angels in your book, but that feather you hold belongs to no bird that I know of in Paris and I found it one day tucked into the blue dark pocket of my coat.'

271. For Yves Klein's new exhibition called *The Void* he purportedly sent out 3,500 white postcards as invitations. He again employed the blue perforated stamp and once more Pierre Restany provided a short text. No one

could gain admission to the exhibition without one of these cards – at least not without paying an elevated charge or penalty.

272. There were guards stationed at the doors to give the exhibition some 'authenticity'. Crowds lined up outside and there was a palpable air of excitement. The outside window was painted blue and blue curtains hung in the corridor where blue cocktails were served.

273. The blue cocktails were a concoction of gin and Cointreau and methylene blue. The methylene turned the drinker's urine blue and in this way they became one with Yves Klein's artwork, which was something of some delight to the artist.

274. He had planned to fly a helicopter over the Place de la Concorde and to drop a blue cloth over the obelisk that stands there like a pointing finger at the sky. This proved to be too expensive so instead he thought he would turn the obelisk blue with light, but permission was not granted for this.

275. Of course there are truth and lies in all of this and maybe numbers have been exaggerated. Yves Klein would go on to claim that the preparation of the exhibition space was something that he worked on in isolation, but at least three of his

friends afterwards said they were there with him creating the experience of 'dematerialised blue'; everything was painted white!

276. I turn the mirror to the wall. I tell her it is so my blue father cannot see us. I do not know if she thinks this is madness. I hold her hand or she holds mine – I know it matters which it is, but as I write this I cannot decide. I lean into her and we kiss. Afterwards I write it all down, the taste of that kiss and how it felt with the palm of her hand pressed to my cheek. I think if I had not written it down I would have forgotten it – which is not to say that it was unremarkable, it's just that kisses are so easily forgotten... not that they have happened but what they were.

277. Maybe Michelle would tell it different from how I tell it. But she would at least say we kissed. I give her the Dalí picture then. She does not open it right away but runs her fingers over the blue shirt-cloth. I had left one of the blue buttons on and her fingers play with that.

278. 'I do not know what this is,' she says. I tell her it is the Dalí picture wrapped in a torn piece of my blue cotton shirt, which had rubbed through to a hole on one sleeve anyway and so would not have been worn again. She does not

mean the picture. She's talking about the kiss and her hand to my cheek. She does not know what *this* is.

279. Maybe it is 'dematerialised love'. Maybe it makes no sense to ask what it is, just as it makes no sense to ask what blue is, for any explanation would leave something important out.

280. Blue is to do with light and the tools of perception. There is not something inherent in the thing that we perceive that may be called blue. It is how the eye reads the reflection of light coming from the surface of the thing. The object absorbs all other colours of light but it reflects or fails to absorb light at the blue end of the spectrum. It is that reflected light that we see and so we call the object blue.

281. But blue is more than this.

282. Blue is a feeling and a time and a memory.

283. Blue is distance and nearness and touch.

284. Blue is an experience and is more than light waves and a specific band on the spectrum. So much more.

285. Henri reads about Yves Klein's new exhibition in the newspaper. There is quite a fuss made of it. There are those who think he is a genius and those that call him 'charlatan'. And someone is complaining about their urine turning blue.

286. The space in the Galerie Colette Allendy has a blue curtain over the outside of the door and a white curtain over the inside. The room itself has been painted white – whitewashed white using a Ripolin enamel roller and paint that has been mixed with the same fixative that Yves Klein used to create his International Klein Blue (IKB). There is nothing in the room except for a glass display case in one corner and a small table placed in the store-front window. Both the table and the display case have also been painted white.

287. This is *The Void* – devoid of anything that might ordinarily be thought of as painting. Devoid of colour – even blue. Devoid of works but not of work.

288. The press thought it might be a hoax and this was a difficult coat to shrug off. It was, for many, too much and as though Yves Klein was now mocking them and maybe, they thought, he had always been mocking them. But one critic declared that the exhibition excited the spirit. Where the blue monochromes had at

least conformed to the idea of art as painting, this was an absence of painting. It was architecture and space.

289. Henri reads in the newspaper that this new exhibition is an absence of art and he does not think he understands. He wants to understand. He asks the woman of the blue flowers if she can make sense of it. 'It seems to be something that must be experienced,' she says. 'Like love, for without the experience of love it does not make sense. And maybe the same is true of God.'

290. 'And it only makes sense for the person or persons actually experiencing it.' Some days she has a feather pinned to the lapel of her coat, sometimes a blue flower, sometimes a knotted piece of twisted blue thread.

291. 'I gave my wedding dress away, for what use is a wedding dress to one who will not again be married? But I withdrew the Tekhelet blue thread. Your grandfather would have wanted me to do that.'

292. The woman of the blue flowers bakes bread for Henri some days and if he is with a customer in the back room she leaves it wrapped in a tea-towel on the desk in the front of the shop.

293. If he is not with a customer and there is no appointment in the ledger, then they break bread together and in that she awakens a memory in Henri. Something he thought he had lost down the back of a sofa somewhere, along with loose change and sewing needles and blue cinema tickets with 'admit one' printed on them.

294. Michelle hangs the Dalí reproduction on the wall opposite her bed. She has other pictures of swallows pinned up there, all of them different and also all somehow the same; all with their wings thrown wide so there is the shape of a blue crescent moon there, the flash of red at their throats and their breasts of white like buttoned-up collarless shirts – except that with Dalí's swallow there is no red.

295. 'Do you think he forgot?' Michelle says. She means Dalí and she means the red that is missing from the blue-inked swallow. 'Do you think he was just painting a swallow from memory and he got the swift flurry of its flight and the flash of white, but he forgot the red? Sometimes when they are in flight it is hard to see the red.'

296. I take her hand, which is something I do now with ease, and I hold up her wrist so she can see her own swallow tattooed on the back of her wrist, just above the strap of her watch. It is as

small as a cuticle on a thumbnail and it's blue
and nothing more than that.

297. And yet it is undoubtedly a swallow. The shape
of its wings and the tail like a two-pronged
fork and that unmistakable blue.

298. Yves Klein pulled on his blue suit, the one that
had been made by the tailor his Aunt Rose,
Tantine, had recommended to him. He noticed
that one sleeve of the jacket was a little frayed. He
examined himself in the mirror and he thought
the blue wool had lost a little of its colour.

299. For his next work of art he decided he would
order a new suit specially. The same blue wool
as before but this time with a blue waistcoat
and a blue tie. With his next work of art, he
planned to *be* the work and so he needed to
dress for the part.

300. Yves Klein wondered for a moment where he
had put the tailor's card. He went first to the
drawer of his writing bureau. It was important
enough he would not have thrown it out, he
thought. Beneath the scrabble of letters and
bills and notes he spied the card, just a corner
of it visible but unquestionably the tailor's card
with the undistinctive and yet recognisable
blue print of the tailor's address.

IV

The Night of Broken Windows
in the Street of Tailors

301. There is in us a need to know. What this is – what life is and what it's for. It can't just be nothing, or chance, nothing more than blue chance. We are born and we live and we die. There has to be something more. That's what we think.

302. And this thing with Michelle, who cannot yet be thirty, and a man who by his own admission was born on 14 May 1957, what is this thing? Is it a device, like a 'love interest' for this novel? These work best if there is a will-they-won't-they element to the relationship. And there is that. So far we have held hands and we have kissed and Michelle has slept in my armchair with a blue stone tucked into her dress pocket.

303. Maybe Michelle is a memory. The one that got away, for we all have those stories, except a writer can rewrite his story and maybe this time she does not get away but stays on the page, fixed in blue ink. (I know that if you are reading this it will be printed in black ink, but I'm writing this with a pen in a notebook with lined pages, so it is as I write something fixed in blue.)

304. Maybe she is more than one memory for there was a girl once who did that thing with her hair and it was so pretty that I have written about it somewhere else. And another girl with eyes that were blue and flecked with broken bits of yellow gold or honeycomb. That can happen in a writer's work, too, that not one girl but several girls are captured in the one character.

305. 'What is this?' Michelle says and she means us and what we are. Then she does that thing with her hair and I notice the sparks of gold in her blue eyes and I say, 'It is what it is.'

306. We are lying fully clothed on the top of her bed and she is holding my hand and we are looking at the wall opposite, where Dalí's blue and white swallow seems impossibly real. And my father is smiling – in my head he is.

307. The woman of blue flowers finds a way to enter Henri's shop without the bell above the door ringing to let him know she is there. She pushes the door only so far that it touches the bell but does not disturb it. Then she slips through the gap, thin as sticks, seeming just to appear suddenly in the back room where Henri is working.

308. He starts each time and snatches for breath. He thinks – just for a moment – she might be one of the angels she once spoke of and maybe under her coat she has wings, tucked up inside with blue and red and yellow feathers.

309. 'Am I going deaf?' Henri says. The woman of blue flowers laughs and she says maybe not deaf but he is certainly going blind. He is hunched over on his stool, a piece of cloth in one hand and a threaded needle in the other. He holds the cloth near to his face and lifted a little towards the light.

310. 'There is a park a short metro ride from here. I went there this morning just to lay down in the sun on the grass. There were a hundred daisies with their heads turned towards the sun and small blue flowers with yellow centres and pink flowers, too. I only noticed these smaller flowers by being so close to them. Each one was as pretty as a painting, a tiny perfect work of art. He does not put His signature to these works. It is enough that they are.'

311. She does not say God but she means God when she talks of the infinite dematerialised

goodness at work in the world. She lays a single blue flower on Henri's open palm.

312. The woman of blue flowers breaks bread with Henri at the start of each day and each time that she does she has another story to tell. The stories all seem to have the same God or goodness in them, drawing Henri's attention to what is beyond the door of his tailor's shop.

313. And as for Yves Klein, he was now an artist in demand. 'Make me a blue sky or a blue sea or a blue flame.' And so he did not have the time to return to Henri's shop, not yet, and the cuffs of his jacket became a little more ragged each day and his red waistcoat lost a little more of the shape it once had.

314. I look through the pages of art books, searching for swallows. There is a work by the French Modernist painter, Edouard Manet. I do not think it is a work that is well known. On a grassy common – with windmills and red roofs in the background and common grazing cattle far off and clouds shifting in a blue sky – two women sit. One is dressed all in black with her head bent over a book; the other is more brightly dressed and she has lowered a red and

yellow parasol so that her white hat is all in the light. The painting is a little blurry, as though it has been executed in a hurry, but there are two sharp-as-knives swallows flying low above the grass. I have seen swallows do that.

315. I buy the book just for that painting and I wrap it in blue cloth – not a torn shirt this time but some dress cloth I have purchased for the purpose. And I leave the book on her pillow. I have put a bookmark in at the page that has the swallows picture on.

316. And Michelle continues to look for blue post-cards for me. She says, 'Close your eyes, shut tight as pinches. And hold out your hands flat as plates.' Then she lays the card in my palm. She does not ever find another of Yves Klein's cards, but there are blue copies and she finds those.

317. In late 1958 Yves Klein was given his first major public commission with the Gelsen-kirchen Musiktheater. He was given the job of decorating the theatre's main entrance and its cloakroom. This was an opportunity to take 'blue' to a much greater scale – not so big as a sky but as big as walls or ceilings.

318. Yves Klein had to work collaboratively with a team of architects and artists. He made big statements on the virtues of collaboration, and the role of collaboration in new art, wanting to wrap the word up in International Klein Blue (IKB) and make it something new. This, at a time in France when the term still carried all the dirty baggage of the war, aroused suspicion in the French newspapers. Hanging it up on the walls of Galerie Colette Allendy or on the walls of Galerie Iris Clert was not enough.

319. On 22 June 1940, Marshal Philippe Pétain signed an armistice with Germany. He spoke on the radio to the nation about a new spirit of collaboration. As part of that collaboration Pétain agreed to hand over the country's 'undesirables'. This included homosexuals and immigrants, traveller communities and, of course, Jews. You can't just paint over that with International Klein Blue (IKB) and think people will forget – no matter how splendid the blue.

320. 'Today there were geese flying in arrow formation in the skies over Paris. Hundreds of them, thousands, and a great cacophony of sound, like badly made trumpets blowing. And

suddenly the bells of Notre-Dame were ringing and somewhere in His blue heaven there must have been dancing.'

321. 'Do angels dance?' says Henri.
'How can they not when there are choirs of angels singing sometimes? And angels dancing is what makes the clouds move and they shake their wings, fluttering like birds, and that explains why sometimes there are feathers of angels adrift in the blue air.'

322. Henri tells the woman of the blue flowers that her bread tastes sweeter today.

323. 'Do not tell me your age, for I know women lie when they do that and you would maybe add a few years so that we are a little nearer to each other and this – whatever this is – might seem then to be nothing unusual.' We are lying on the top of her bed, still fully clothed, and Michelle has propped the book open at the Manet painting, the book sitting at the foot of the bed. 'Swallows come and they go, flying to always be in a blue sky,' she says.

324. What if I can make a small change to what I have just written? What if we are not fully

clothed but Michelle has slipped out of her dress because in Paris today it is warm as ovens? What if she is lying next to me in her underwear and the windows are thrown wide and the curtains hang still and do not move for the air does not move, and swallows sit panting on the wires outside Michelle's window, hanging breathless in Paris's blue sky?

325. I want to tell her that I love her. But that would be like a handclap to frighten swallows out of the air. Instead I tell Michelle that I once held a dead swallow in the cup of my hands. There must have been a sharp handclap to make it fall out of the sky as it had. I cup my hands together as though I am still holding the dead bird. 'And I wished it was not dead and I closed my eyes and blew into the blue bird's red-masked face.' I blow into the cup of my hands.
'And did it suddenly take breath and fly up out of your prayer palms?'
It didn't as you know, but I let Michelle think that it did and that is a little like saying 'I love you'.

326. And I read somewhere that Yves Klein did not take a patent out on his special blue as I'd earlier said he did. It was something else that he filed for. It was a special protection he took

out so that no one could produce copies of his blue paintings and call them theirs. Such a protection could only last for five years. Then everyone and anyone could put their signatures to God's blue sky.

327. But then today I read that he *did* take out a patent on his special blue. The patent has a number – 63471. It was taken out in May 1960 protecting Yves Klein's rights in connection with the invention of International Klein Blue (IKB). Notice that word 'invention'. It says Yves Klein invented a colour, but this is not true for he merely worked on a process to stop the colour from deteriorating in its journey from pigment to painted canvas.

328. One of the paintings he produced for the Gelsenkirchen Musiktheater was seven metres high by twenty metres long, a ripple effect in International Klein Blue (IKB), like a whole river running through the lobby of the theatre. Indeed, two rivers, for he produced two of these works.

329. 'There was sunlight on glass today, blinding like gold, flashing like a hand waving, His hand. I stopped what I was doing and paid at-

tention to what He wanted me to notice. There was a child, a small boy, and he had fallen in the street and his knee was grazed. I knelt down beside the boy and told him it would be all right. I tore a strip from my petticoat and bound up his knee. You see, I thought I was helping him but when I looked into the boy's blue eyes I could see that he was helping me.'

330. Henri has his nose pressed to the pages of his book. He had recently been praying and it was a prayer he had used to say when he was a boy. He'd stumbled over the words and so now he is looking the prayer up in his book – which is really God's book. Henri has not done this for a long time. He glances up at the woman of the blue flowers and she is a little out of focus so he is not sure she is even there.

331. 'I will go with you,' says the woman of the blue flowers. 'It does not hurt. And it will not take above an hour. A small test to discover how bad your eyes are. And once he knows' – and Henri understands that the 'he' this time is not God but is the optician – 'once he knows then he can begin the task of grinding the lenses for your particular glasses.'

332. The optician puts a pair of heavy glasses balanced on the bridge of Henri's nose and into these frames he inserts small glass discs – some of them tinted blue or rose or yellow; some of them clear – and he asks Henri to read letters from a chart on his wall, as though he is a small child at school and he does not know words yet.

333. And there is a moment when everything on the chart is sharp as pins, even the letters that are small as ink-blue ants.

334. Maybe when the old no longer see colours the way that the young do, so that colour is not fresh and new any more but is something dirty, then all they need is to be fitted for glasses. (It must not be thought that Henri is old, just that his eyes are.) The effect on Henri is transformational and he sees the world anew, as though God has remade it for him. And he sees the goodness in it, the goodness that the woman of the blue flowers has been talking about for almost a month.

335. Yves Klein tucked the tailor's card into the pocket of his red waistcoat, the one that was losing its shape more and more. He checked

his watch on its gold chain. He patted the pocket of his waistcoat again. There'd be time enough for buying new suits and shoes and gloves when this commission was done, he thought. He was at work with sponges soaked in International Klein Blue (IKB), fixing them to an enormous canvas that would take ten men to lift into place in the Gelsenkirchen Musiktheater lobby.

336. And there were other paintings he had to complete for an exhibition in America and another one in Paris. It was not enough for these to be blue. They had to be more than that.

337. Now when I think of that story of the dead swallow in my hands I do not think it was dead. The story has changed and with it the memory has changed, too. Love can do that. Love can make us see blue as blue again and rose as rose, gold as gold – love can do that even for the old. Now when I hold that dead swallow of memory in my hands and breathe on it, it wakes from sleep and flies up out of my hands.

338. And there's a question I do not ask of Michelle and it is not because I know the answer but because I do not yet know the question. My

father laughs as I write that. I only know that there is a question. It is a riddle, I know. Michelle pins another blue postcard to my bedroom wall, a little crookedly but no matter for it is not the right blue.

339. Some days I say to Michelle not to go into work today. Never mind that the man at the next stall will nod and wink and tap one finger down the side of his nose, thinking he knows what's what. 'Paris is a city for lovers,' I tell her. There's a café I want to show her, with a blue-and-white-striped awning and tables on the pavement outside. They know me there but they do not know me with Michelle.

340. It's like skipping school when she says yes. We dress in clean clothes. I ask her if she will wear the white dress with the blue flowers that she wore before. I do not ask for this dress because I cannot think of another dress to put her in. The dress has a particular memory for me for it is a real dress and once it was worn by a real girl and some of that girl I have put into Michelle.

341. It's confusing. I understand that. Like juggling ideas in my head. Like the man at the foot of the steps at *Le Passage de la Sorcière* in

Montmartre with his silver egg cups and his wooden ball. And he shifts that ball around in such a blur that I wonder if he sometimes loses track of where it is. And then the ball is not under the cup he expects it to be under and so he loses some money but smiles to let you think this was all a part of the trick; and when he smiles the blue stone in his tooth sparks.

342. Henri has two pairs of glasses. One is for reading and the man at the optician's says Henri should read only in strong light and not by candle or gaslight. The second pair is for looking at distance and everything is so sharp he can see each leaf of a tree and each blade of grass down by the river long before he is standing on the grass; he can even see the colour of men's eyes when they pass him in the street and they are sometimes blue or green or brown.

343. And one morning, when the woman of the blue flowers is breaking bread with Henri, she turns to him and says maybe he should now be telling her stories in the way that she has been telling them to him.

344. 'I make suits for men, young and old, and in secret I sew a blue twisted Tekhelet thread

somewhere into the trousers so they will be lucky.' Henri laughs when he says it and the woman of the blue flowers laughs, too. Henri, when he hears her laughing, thinks the woman is maybe not so old as she was.

345. Yves Klein had ideas that he said were his own but maybe they were ideas that were in the air around him and he had merely breathed them in. That can happen, I think. Yves Klein was thinking beyond the blue. He was thinking of sculptures in fire and water and something else.

346. It was a continuation of his pursuit of the immaterial. It was blue-sky thinking. It was a work of collaboration, this thinking. And there it was again, that dirty word that the French recoil from.

347. Michelle and I are sitting outside at the café with the blue-and-white-striped awning. The sun is high in the sky and so we cannot be hidden. She does that thing with her hair again: the catch and drag of her index finger and then tucking the miscreant lock of hair behind her ear. 'I see, I see,' says my father, as though I have asked him if he does. It is a signature move, like Yves Klein putting his

name to the sky, the same finger. 'Just like your mother,' my father says, but though the move is something other women do, I think this one is Michelle's and hers only.

348. 'What?' she says. I am smiling, perhaps. Of course I am. Who wouldn't be smiling to see what she just did. 'What?' she says again. A man walks past and he is not smiling. Indeed he wears a blue-punched frown. I do not think he has seen what Michelle just did with her hair.

349. 'It is something you do without even thinking, without knowing what it is. An unconscious piece of poetry so beautiful it would somehow fail if I was to put it into words, if it could not be seen.' That is what I think, or what my father thinks, but not what I say. Instead I tell her I am happy, 1,001 blue-helium-filled-balloons happy.

350. Henri and the woman of the blue flowers close up the shop some mornings, just for an hour. Henri puts a sign on the door to say he will be back soon. They walk to the river on those days; there's a bench there that they call their own; or they go to a shop where they sell crois-

sants and coffee. Henri orders for them both and they sit and watch the world pass by.

351. 'There was a night when all the windows in the street were broken. Stones thrown into the shop, stones the shape of hard fists, and hammers tap-tapping at the glass. We lived above the shop then. My father said he would go out to see what it was. My mother cried to him "no" and begged him not to go out into the blue-black thumping dark.'

352. It is another morning and they are breaking bread and saying prayers together. The woman of the blue flowers is quiet and listening.

353. 'But he would not be stopped, not even when his father – my grandfather – told him he should wait. Afterwards, when the blue light of a new day fell on the street – not like a blessing but like a curse, like a sin when the curtain is pulled back to reveal it – then we could all see what the night had brought. My father lay crumpled in the road. He could not see out of more than one eye and all his fingers were broken. I do not think he was ever the father he had once been from that day on.'

354. 'I was a tailor from that night. I was the tailor my father could not be again, not with his fingers all crooked like the claws of a crow, a blue-backed, black-beaked crow. I was a tailor and I was twelve.'

355. The woman of the blue flowers weeps.

356. Though the *Air Architecture* ideas – for Yves Klein's thinking included not just sculpture in fire and water but also in air – though the ideas were not his own but shared, in April 1958 Yves Klein took out a patent on them. He began making sketches for them in blue pencil on blank newsprint paper.

357. And light, he wanted to use, projected blue light. And sound and movement. His mind was like a sponge, soaking up the ideas that were everywhere. Maybe he really believed they were his own, just as he once believed the sky above Nice with his name invisibly attached to it was his greatest artwork.

358. 'I know it is not quite what you are looking for, but it is close.' (She does not know that I have found what I have been looking for here at the table pulled out on to the pavement and people

passing by so they can see me with Michelle.)
She withdraws from her handbag a postcard.
It is blue – the same blue that was on that first
postcard and the corners of the blue made
round so it could be the same or a copy. On the
back the card carries a blue stamp – not Yves
Klein's blue-lie stamp – but a blue République
Française stamp, the head of the republic with
her laurelled head facing right and the blue sun
coming up.

359. 'Her hair, do you see. Her blue hair is tucked
behind her ear. That's what you do,' I tell her.

360. Michelle leans towards me and we kiss. It
is something and nothing. I look over my
shoulder to see if someone else in the street has
noticed. But, as you know, this is all a blue
fictive dream and so it would be a surprise to
me and to you if anyone had noticed.

361. The woman of the blue flowers pushes the door
of Henri's shop just so it touches the bell, then
she slips through the gap and surprises Henri
again. He is in the back stitching the arms to a
jacket. He is not wearing his glasses and there
is no light to see by.

362. He looks up before she speaks, as if he has heard her step at the door. She looks thinner somehow. Not thin like girls on the covers of magazines, but thin like cloth when it is a veil worn by a bride. To Henri's unbespectacled eyes that is how the woman of the blue flowers looks. And younger she looks also, young like his mother looks whenever he remembers her.

363. 'Have you worked through the night?' she asks. He does not nod or make any other sign to show that that is exactly what he has done. She has a pot of coffee in one hand and a loaf of bread in the other. She sits down on the floor and pulls cups and spoons and bottles of milk from the pockets of her coat. And blue feathers are pulled out also, blue feathers that are also white and very like that first feather she showed him and she said it was the feather of an angel.

364. 'There was something good that morning after the night of broken windows. A girl in the street was cradling my father's head in her lap. She was wiping the blood from his face and saying that she was sorry even though it was nothing of her doing. She came to the house above the shop every day for a month to ask

after my father. I noticed that she wore a ring on her wedding finger – not gold or silver, but a blue twisted thread. A Tekhelet thread.'

365. 'My mother never answered the door to the girl. Nor did my father when he was able to walk about the house again. I was the one who answered the door to her and I was the one who passed her news of how my father was doing. She fiddled with the blue thread ring on her finger, as though she wanted me to notice it.'

366. 'I did not tell my father of her visits and my mother said I was not to speak of her to anyone. That's when I first stitched a blue thread into the hem of a man's trousers. I did it after dark, when my father and my grandfather were both asleep. I crept downstairs and in the dark I twisted the thread in my fingers and pushed it through the eye of a needle – my grandfather had shown me how to do that even with my eyes closed, so the dark was no obstacle to what I did – and I opened up a hem and stitched the thread inside.'

367. 'Put your glasses on, Henri,' says the woman of the blue flowers. She pours two cups of coffee,

adds milk and breaks the loaf of bread and gives thanks to her God. Henri gives thanks to his.

368. 'I had forgotten all about that girl with the blue thread ring until now,' Henri says.

369. Yves Klein was also at this time producing his *Anthropometries*. This was the name he gave to a series of works involving female nude models daubed in International Klein Blue (IKB) paint and rolling about on canvas. The blue impressions they left on the cloth were the works and the performance of the creation of the works was also art.

370. Then he read that someone else was doing something the same – another artist in France. The unknown artist was reported as using nude models in an unspecified way to make artworks, though not necessarily using Yves Klein's special blue.

371. Yves Klein was furious. He wanted ownership of this idea to be asserted as his. Just as he claimed that the term 'monochrome painting' was his and he forbade a fellow artist from using the term about his own work, works that

were not blue but explored other colours in the same monochrome experiment.

372. He painted discs in International Klein Blue (IKB), and cubes he painted blue; and walls and floors and doors – whole rooms. He painted a three-dimensional globe blue and it hung on an invisible thread and spun like the world turning.

373. The woman of the blue flowers is not as bent as she was. That is what Henri thinks when he puts on his glasses again. And there is no noise in the back of her throat when she drops to kneel on the floor or when she rises again.

374. Henri wonders if time's arrow can fly backwards as surely as it flies forwards. Maybe if the flight feathers are blue and white – the feathers of an angel's wings?

375. 'The thing I remember most about the night of the broken windows in the Street of Tailors is clinging on to my father's leg, trying to hold my father back as much as my mother's begged "no" should have held him back from going out into the street. I remember my hand pressed to his inside leg and how warm it was

there and safe. But my father shook me from his leg and went out anyway.'

376. 'I do not think you can stop the inevitable. Not with love or need, not even with lies.'
The woman of the blue flowers pushes blue and white angel feathers into Henri's pockets. 'Maybe,' she says.

377. I find another swallow painting. It is a second work by Dalí. A finished sketch for a painting he maybe never did: *The Motionless Swallow – Study for Still Life Fast Moving*. It shows a swallow hanging still in the air, hovering in a captured moment with its shadow thrown beneath it and to the side and on to a wall. The shadow seems to dart and dive in a way that the 'living' swallow doesn't. In the background clouds break open to reveal an intense blue sky.

378. Michelle recognises it as a Dalí as soon as I show her the page in a book. She says, 'One swallow does not a summer make, but maybe two…?' and she laughs then at the small joke she has made. I do not tell her that she is making my summer. I look up at the blue of the sky that affirms that it is indeed summer.

379. It is a book of little worth other than the Dalí picture, so we agree to carefully tear the plate from the book so we can pin it alongside the other Dalí swallow on Michelle's bedroom wall. Then we undress and lie down on the top of her bed and swallows turn the air blue with their swift swooping and swinging.

380. Blue is God's colour. That's what artists once believed. It is why the infinite heavens are blue and the endless sea and the cloth worn by the Blessed Virgin.

381. And when Moses saw God in the burning bush, we cannot think that the bush was red with fire but was rather blue-flamed, like the tongues of skinks – a lizard from the antipodes and it shows its blue tongue as an act of defence, a warning to its enemies: God is here. Stand well back or burn.

382. Henri with his glasses on sees the world sharp again and blue, but he chooses more and more not to wear his glasses.

383. Instead, Henri chooses the blue indefinite haze where ghosts move on slippered feet and angel feathers fill the pockets of his coat and the

pockets of his jacket and his trousers – feathers where once there were stones.

384. And God, Henri's God, is come back to him and is blue-flamed again.

385. And once the woman of the blue flowers, she was a little shorter than she is now. Henri is sure of that, as sure as he can be of anything when he is not wearing his glasses. Now she walks straighter and there's a spring in her step which is like dancing.

386. And Henri catches music in the air when the woman of the blue flowers is near and he does not at first know that the music is his own singing.

387. Yves Klein created a work called *Zones of Immaterial Pictorial Sensibility*. He sold these 'zones' for gold and issued certificates to the art lovers who parted with their gold. Then, if the art lover agreed to burn the certificate, Yves Klein agreed to throw half the gold into the blue waters of the Seine.

388. There are pictures in black and white of Yves Klein dropping gold leaf on to the waters of

the Seine. We can only imagine the gold and the blue.

389. Yves Klein is dressed smartly in the pictures. He wears a shirt and bow tie and a suit underneath his light-coloured coat. It is the blue suit that Henri made for him and the coat is to hide the cuffs of the jacket, which are soft and threaded.

390. It was time that Yves Klein returned to Henri's shop and time he was measured for another suit. He had been lucky so far and so he thought he would like a second suit exactly the same blue – like the back of a swallow – and with a red waistcoat for summer and a blue waistcoat for winter.

391. 'Do you think it was a real swallow that he saw?' Michelle asks me, pointing to the new Dalí picture on the wall. 'Or do you think it is like the blue splash of ink and it is something he painted out of his head, something of a dream?'

392. I have seen birds displayed in museums just like that second Dalí painting, hanging on a thin thread that in some lights is almost invisible so that the bird with its wings spread open seems to be levitating, or dropping from the blue sky

and somehow held in that one eternal moment before hitting the ground.

393. 'Maybe it is something real *and* imagined,' I say. 'Things can be both, I think.' Michelle laughs and she leans into me and kisses my cheek. 'Like us?' she says. I look into the blue of her eyes, blue flecked with honeycomb – the Seine littered with Yves Klein's gold leaf. 'Real and imagined, yes, like us.'

394. Yves Klein sold three of his 'immaterial zones' and, as promised and with great show he completed the ritual transfer by throwing half of the gold into the Seine. With the other half he constructed an ex-voto offering to St Rita of Cascia. This second act was something he did quietly. It is a box that he gifted to a nun in a blue shawl at the monastery in Cascia.

395. In the box, a sumptuous reliquary, there are three upper compartments, one filled with blue pigment the colour of International Klein Blue (IKB), one filled with a rose-coloured pigment and one filled with gold leaf.

396. Another lower compartment holds three small ingots of gold from the sale of his

'immaterial zones' carefully arranged on a bed of blue pigment.

397. Between these two compartments there is a further compartment that holds a handwritten prayer to St Rita of Cascia – written in blue ink, the colour of a Tekhelet thread.

398. A reliquary usually contains the physical remains of a saint or holy martyr – pieces of hair or bone or skin, parts of clothing they once wore. Yves Klein's reliquary holds the constituent parts of his art: blue and rose and gold.

399. The ex-voto offering was not discovered and verified to be the work of Yves Klein until 1979 – long after his death. By this time his reputation had been established and International Klein Blue (IKB) was something that was recognised across the art world.

400. If things here are a little out of time maybe it has something to do with the direction of time's arrow, which in fiction can be flighted with an angel's feathers – blue and white – and does not need to travel forward but can flip backwards if it must. Memory is like that, too.

V

One, Two, Three, Four
Leaps into the Void

401. 'How long?' Michelle says. I do not know what she means and neither does my father. 'How long is a summer?' Then I get it. She's talking about the swallows nesting on the undersides of the roof outside her window. She wants to know how long the sky will be blue enough for those swallows. She wants to know when the tide of blue will recede taking the swallows with it.

402. Summers, looking back, have sometimes stretched beyond horizons; sometimes they have passed in a blink. I do not have an answer for Michelle except that I wish this summer would hold its blue and not ever let it go.

403. No, I don't really wish that. But I shall be sorry when this summer is over and looking back it will not be one of those endless summers – not even though it is written down in a book and can be lived over and over. It will be a gone-in-a-blink summer and the blue of the sky will not look so blue as it does at this moment.

404. Henri hears the bell of the shop ring. He brushes lint from the front of his waistcoat, adjusts his glasses and steps out from the back of the shop. It is Yves Klein returned – as swallows will return, as readers may return to these pages, again and again. Henri smiles,

noticing the frayed cuffs of the blue jacket that had once been pieces of cloth laid out on his table in the shop.

405. 'It's a lucky suit,' declares Yves Klein. 'I should like another just like it. The same blue and the same cut. And a red waistcoat the same and a second waistcoat that is the colour of the suit. And I need this new suit to be the same lucky as the first.'

406. Henri ushers Yves Klein into the back of the shop. He must take new measurements, he says, for we all change through time and he can see that Yves Klein is a little heavier than before – though he does not say that. Luck in a blue suit can do that to a man.

407. Yves Klein strips down to his underwear and emerges from behind the curtain of the changing area. He is taller, perhaps, or he holds himself with a greater assurance than he once did. He notices the newspaper clippings on the wall and he nods at his own blue-lit fame.

408. 'I have a plan for something even greater than all the rest. Not blue this time but beyond blue. A leap of the imagination and the spirit. A leap into the infinite.'

409. Henri runs the tape measure up Yves Klein's inside leg. He remembers his father on that night of the broken windows in the street of tailors. Remembers the blue-black bruises of his father's eye afterwards and his father's fingers curled into the claws of dead birds.

410. 'That's why I need the new suit. Not that I don't have other suits, but this suit must be especially lucky and blue, splendid and catching the eye the way that swallows catch the eye when they dip and dive to the level of the streets in Paris. Have you seen them?'

411. It was around this time that the Russians were planning to send a man into space. They had sent Laika, the dog, a few years earlier. It did not survive the flight for they did not yet have the technology to bring the dog back successfully. I have a Romanian blue stamp with a picture of Laika on it, an unremarkable stray mongrel except remarkably it once orbited the Earth.

412. I try to picture Michelle in a shapeless winter coat standing at the bottom of the Eiffel Tower selling her postcards and CDs and old books that she has unloaded from a Peugeot 4DA van, circa 1952, and arranged on three wooden trestle tables. I try but I cannot. Michelle belongs in blue and white summer dresses with

her hair loose and on one side tucked behind her ear.

413. The man at the next stall, I can picture him in gloves and hat and scarf. There is something more permanent about him. As though he has always been there and always will be. Like Yves Klein's blue monochromes, which are just as blue today as they were when he painted them.

414. The woman of the blue flowers claps her hands and she says it is good to see Henri so lit up again. She makes him stop for a break and offers him coffee and bread and prayers.

415. Henri tells her about the night 'they' came for his family. It was expected and so they each had a packed suitcase of belongings – even his father whose fingers were claws. The order declared they were to wear yellow stars fixed to their coats – their stars were so well stitched that they could almost be worn with pride. Then, at the last minute, Henri was pushed into the blue-black dark of a concealed cupboard behind a bookcase in the shop and told to stay there quiet as the dead.

416. 'I do not think I even breathed or thought or was. And now it is as though I am brought back from the dead, but I have heard that the

dead do not ever do that, do not ever really come back.' The woman of the blue flowers nods and this day she does not eat her bread or drink her coffee.

417. On 12 January 1960 Yves Klein performed his first *Leap into the Void*. The morning was cold and the sky held nothing of the blue that he once signed his name to. He leaped from the second storey of a house belonging to the gallery owner Colette Allendy. He was tremendously excited afterwards and breathless. He reported to everyone on the failure of gravity with his successful performance of levitation. Space was not something to be conquered by scientists and rockets and cosmonauts, he declared, but by artists.

418. Yves Klein was not wearing his lucky blue suit for this first *Leap into the Void*. He suffered a sprained ankle and walked with a limp for several days following the feat.

419. 'There were no goodbyes, not from my mother or grandfather. Just the push of my father's hand on my back and his hissed instructions thrown after me into the dark. I never saw them again, nor ever heard their voices coming to me from the next room. They simply disappeared, into the blue nothing of history. Maybe their

names are written down somewhere in one of "their" books. Maybe.'

420. Then she is speaking. 'They say that if you catch a falling angel's feather before it touches the ground, then you can make a wish – any wish at all – and the wish will be granted unto you.' Henri looks at the woman of the blue flowers, not wearing his glasses but seeing her through a blurry and blue veil. 'Remember I told you I once had such a feather that I found; well I have another in my pocket and I caught it one day, snatched it out of the air, and it still holds its wish for I never made one. Just maybe I can gift this feather with the wish to you.'

421. The woman of the blue flowers dips her hand into the folds of her dress and produces from a hidden pocket a feather of the same blue and white she had once shown Henri – it looks exactly the same to Henri's eyes, whether he is wearing his glasses or not.

422. It was talked about, Yves Klein's *Leap into the Void*. Within his circle it was talked about. There were those who accepted it was true and those who doubted it. Yves Klein spoke of it in religious terms, as though it was a matter of faith and a trust in God. It was for him a leap into the blue, which is infinite and without boundary.

423. The critic Pierre Restany urged him to perform the *Leap* a second time and for there to be witnesses who would testify afterwards that it was truth. It was at this time that Yves Klein returned to the tailor called Henri and ordered a new blue suit, a lucky suit with a blue Tekhelet thread stitched into the trousers, though he did not know about the thread.

424. 'The swallows are gathering,' Michelle says. Outside her window, strung out on telephone wires reaching in zig-zag stitches between the buildings are hundreds of swallows chattering excitedly about blue skies and the sun of faraway places. It is a dream in their small heads then and a journey of thousands of miles is no obstacle to making that dream a reality. And the swallows are also gathered on the wall of Michelle's bedroom, pictures of them, not a square inch of wallpaper showing, hundreds of swallows darting this way and that across her bedroom wall.

425. She kisses me then and it is all the kisses I had as a boy rolled into one and there are no words to describe that kiss, for how can words do justice to something so elusive? I have tried to describe a kiss before and in words it loses something of what it was, just as blue pigment mixed with

a binder loses something of its wonder in the transfer to canvas – at least before Yves Klein.

426. Elusive because it belongs to memory, which is like something written on the surface of blue water and it never stays still; elusive because it belongs in imagination – in my imagination and in yours if you are reading this. Remember how kisses once were for you, how they are for you now? One day those kisses will lose all shape and definition. They will continue to exist, fixed in memory, but something in them will be lost, too.

427. Henri takes the feather offered to him by the woman of the blue flowers. She lays it gentle in his hand, as though it is something so fragile that breath could break it, as though it is something sacred – as blue used to be sacred and reserved for angels and saints and the most holy. He does not close his hand but pulls the feather slowly towards him. He opens the pocket of his waistcoat, where once there might have been a watch, and he drops the feather into the pocket. He pats it softly and thinks on the wish he will make.

428. He cuts the shape of Yves Klein out of pieces of blue wool cloth, holding his breath from the start of the cut until his scissors have reached

the full length of it. He does all this in the near dark with the woman of blue flowers watching over him from the door. He moves quickly and easily round the table, pressing the cloth flat with the brush of his hand, careful not to wipe away the criss-cross marks of his tailor's chalk. And the woman of the blue flowers holds her breath the same as Henri and lets it go again when he closes his scissors and looks at what he has done.

429. 'Can you close the windows?' Michelle says. 'It's a little cooler today, I think.' We are lying on the bed listening to the swallows bitching about sunnier days. We are not undressed as we were before, but are lying next to each other in our clothes. Still it feels cold. I get up to do as she asks and looking up I see the sky is losing its blue and, though I will miss the swallows when they go, I wish them gone to skies that deserve them.

430. Yves Klein agreed to make the *Leap* again. This time he'd be wearing a new suit – made by a tailor whose suits are lucky, though Yves Klein did not tell anyone this. He would make the *Leap* again and it would be a quiet show but this time there'd be a record, proof that a man can hang in space without the help of science. It'd be a performance, one of the most

important events of Yves Klein's life and all the world would bear witness to it. He made a plan, walked the streets of Paris looking for the perfect location.

431. Henri tacks the blue wool cloth to pieces of interface to stiffen the fabric and so it will hang right. This will be a suit to eclipse all other suits, he thinks. This will be the last word in suits. He holds a piece of cloth in the air, imagining what it will be with Yves Klein in it. He pins the pieces to the leather mannequin body and, as he did once before, he holds on to the end of the sleeve, looking into the mirror. It is as though he is holding the hand of Yves Klein, but in his head he is remembering how he once held the hand of his father just the same.

432. 'There were stories that came after they were gone. Stories too cruel to be true. Except that when the war was over what could not be true was proven to be true. So many men and women and children, all of them disappeared. Nothing of them to say prayers over, nothing but blue smoke adrift in the Heavens. Whole streets disappeared. Like the Street of Tailors here in Paris and it is gone now and this is the last shop where you can have a suit made in what was that street.'

433. The woman of the blue flowers looks more and more like a girl. To Henri she does. Like the girl cradling his beaten father in the street on that night of broken windows in the rue des Tailleurs. And she came to the door to ask after his father and Henri was the only one who heard her knock and the only one who answered the door. And didn't she wear a Tekhelet thread ring about her finger? He thinks she did but his memory fails him a little – even though he is not old.

434. We count the age of a man in years, but maybe Henri is old in another way. Maybe a man can be old even if he does not have the weight of years pulling him down and down to earth. Maybe there is a force other than gravity that weighs heavy on his shoulders and carrying this grave weight can age a man even where there are not so many years. Maybe it is the same thing, this 'blue gravity', the same thing that Yves Klein talked of when it failed to let him fall and allowed him to levitate.

435. 'I hate the cold,' says Michelle. 'It feels more real than the warmth, more real than the sun and blue skies.' I know what she means; my father nods to show he knows, too.

436. 'Cold is something hard,' she says. 'Like truth. They say that, don't they? Cold hard truth. I

am not sure that I like truth when it is like that. If it comes down to it I think I prefer lies – the white and the blue and black lies. There is some soft comfort in lies. We can be together in lies and together always.' I do not wish to take issue with what she is saying. I do not want to contest her lies with my fiction, which is sometimes nearer to truth even when it is a lie.

437. Michelle is like those swallows perched on the telephone wires outside her window. She is chattering and winnowing her wings and preparing for a journey of thousands of miles, sleeping on the wing and letting the air carry her off to those African skies where the blue is so sharp it hurts to look at it for too long.

438. He found his street. It was located in the Paris suburb of Fontenay-aux-Roses. Standing in the rue Gentil-Bernard Yves Klein pictured the whole thing in his head. The street was quiet as an empty church and there was a stone ledge he could imagine throwing himself from and the sky above on the day he visited was blue and he reached up and put his signature to that sky, too.

439. He used fingers to construct a frame, the shape of a photograph. He shifted it this way and that and filled that frame with Yves Klein leaping

from the stone ledge and held in the air. Like the stories of the saints that his Aunt Rose, Tantine, told him when he was a boy. Stories of St Rita lifting off the ground and floating in the blue air – for when his aunt told the story they were in Nice and there the air is almost always blue.

440. And Aunt Rose, Tantine, told Yves Klein of St Joseph of Cupertino who wore chains under his loose-fitting clothes, chains so heavy he could not float away. There is a painting of St Joseph by Ludovico Mazzanti and St Joseph is not wearing his chains in the painting for he is adrift in the air. And it looks like falling and like flying both at the same time. Just over St Joseph's shoulder the clouds have broken open and the sky is the colour of International Klein Blue (IKB).

441. In the finger frame that Yves Klein made and held up to the sky he could see himself, exactly like St Joseph in Ludovico Mazzanti's painting. The same held moment of falling and flying and the same blue sky over his shoulder.

442. Henri waits for Yves Klein to undress behind the curtain of his back room. He has told the woman of blue flowers that Yves Klein is coming for his fitting so she has not appeared

this morning with her offering of coffee and
bread. Henri has almost finished the suit – it
is always a little easier when he is making a
suit for someone whose shape he has become
familiar with, even when that body has altered
by small degrees.

443. There are only a few minor adjustments to be
made. He marks the cloth with his blue tailor's
chalk and he nods and smiles and says the
suit is almost perfect. Yves Klein looks at his
reflection in the mirror and he knows the suit
is better even than the last one. 'Even luckier,'
he says under his breath and it is a prayer and
a wish both at the same time.

444. The time between my visits to Michelle's room
and lying next to her on the bed looking at the
still blue swallows on her wall and the restless
blue swallows outside her window, well, there
are spaces in that time, spaces that stretch and
widen. Sometimes I do not see her for days.
Not even at the foot of the Eiffel Tower selling
postcards and old books and CDs beside the
man at the next stall who is now wearing a
scarf in the early mornings.

445. On 19 October 1960 Yves Klein staged the first
of two jumps from the stone ledge of 3 rue Gentil-
Bernard. He had arranged for a photographer to

capture the moment. He is pictured in full leap, his arms outstretched like the wings of a bird, his hair blown back from his forehead and he carries all the confidence of one who knows the air will not let him fall. He was wearing the blue suit that Henri had finished altering. He looks smart in his suit and tie and such smartness only adds to the sense of spectacle we witness in the photograph.

446. He repeated the leap less than a week later on 25 October 1960. He was dressed the same in the photographs for this second leap – a hidden blue Tekhelet thread sewn into the waistband of his trousers. The street was empty except for a cyclist at the far end cycling away from the miracle of Yves Klein's *Leap into the Void*. A train also passed the end of the leafy street – maybe someone on the train looked out and saw Yves Klein hanging in the air.

447. He produced his own newspaper to mark the event. It was freely available from all Paris news kiosks. The front cover showed the black and white picture of Yves Klein in mid-leap – not unlike the Mazzanti painting of St Joseph with the blue sky breaking open over his shoulder.

448. Inside the pages of his newspaper Yves Klein wrote with a fervour of the mystical role of the

artist and how art, not science, would be the thing to conquer blue space. The picture was proof of what he wrote.

449. The woman of the blue flowers holds Henri's arm when they go out walking. He leans a little more on her each day. They walk by the river, sometimes as far as the Eiffel Tower with its single finger pointing up at the sky. 'So high it almost touches Heaven,' says Henri one day.

450. The woman of the blue flowers slips feathers into all of his pockets and all of them are angel feathers. Maybe they all have wishes waiting to be granted, too.

451. 'I should like to one day stand at the top of the tower and reach one hand up towards where my father and mother and grandfather are,' Henri says. She looks at him and the blue of her eyes is so deep that he wonders how he did not notice it before.

452. 'Have you seen Michelle?' I ask the man at the next stall. He shakes his head and he makes his hands into a bird, his thumbs linked and his fingers like spread wings. He flaps his fingers lifting his two-handed bird into the blue sky and then he claps his hands suddenly and shows them empty as though the bird has magically disappeared.

453. The picture of Yves Klein's *Leap into the Void* is a marvellous lie. Maybe the day was blue and maybe he believed that he floated on the air, even for the briefest of moments. Flying and falling can feel the same until the landing. But he knew for sure that the picture was a manufactured lie.

454. Henri has Yves Klein's newspaper pinned with the other pictures on the wall of his back room. He says it is a miracle and he says it is God's doing. He speaks to the blue-black shadows behind boxes in his workshop and he says he is speaking with God again.

455. The photographer of Yves Klein's *Leap into the Void* took two pictures. The first was of the near empty street with the train at the end and the cyclist with his back to the camera. The second was of Yves Klein throwing himself into the blue; but below Yves Klein were ten strong men holding on to a stretched tarpaulin ready to catch him. The published photograph is a clever montage of the two pictures.

456. Nobody today, seeing the picture of Yves Klein's *Leap into the Void* believes he can levitate, that the air does not let him fall but holds him in a blue and tender embrace. We all

know the photograph is a lie. Art is allowed to lie, it seems, just as writing is.

457. Henri sweeps the floor of his shop, the front room and the back. He arranges the scissors and his measure and all his pins and needles. Lays them down as if for inventory. He folds away the bolt of blue cloth that he'd used for Yves Klein's lucky suit, everything neat and tidy as though he is expecting visitors – as though his father might walk through the door and wish to inspect his son's workplace.

458. The woman of the blue flowers nods her head in approval of the shop in its new clothes and not a pin out of place. She holds Henri's coat out for him to slip his arms into – she is surely taller, he thinks.

459. 'My name is not Henri,' he tells the woman of the blue flowers. 'My father said I should use that name so "they" would not know me for what I was and so "they" would not take me away as they did him. My name is Hayyim, which means "life".'

460. 'It's been a few days,' I tell the man at the next stall. He shrugs. 'What can I say?' he says. He pretends to juggle cups or cards on the table in front of him, lifts one and declares, 'She is

never where you expect or want her to be.' He reminds me in that moment of the man with the blue lapis stone in his tooth who sits at the bottom of the steps at *Le Passage de la Sorcière* in Montmartre taking money off the tourists.

461. On 12 April 1961 Yuri Alekseyevich Gagarin completed the first manned trip into space, flying more than 110 miles above the planet in its orbit. It was a moment of historic significance. His spacecraft, Vostok 1, successfully circled the Earth and returned. On seeing Earth from on high Yuri Gagarin declared: 'Земля синяя, как это замечательно удивительно!' ('The Earth is blue... how wonderful, it is amazing!')

462. When Yves Klein read those words in the newspaper, he cried for joy and then took credit for what Yuri Gagarin had said. After all, it is what he'd been about with his art. And hadn't he already painted a globe in International Klein Blue (IKB) and exhibited it in a gallery in Krefeld, Germany?

463. Hayyim's coat pockets are stuffed with feathers, his jacket pockets, too, and his trouser pockets. All feathers, white and somehow blue at the same time. Angels' feathers. The woman of the blue flowers takes his hand and she asks him if he has decided on a wish.

464. They walk along the side of the river until they reach the Eiffel Tower that seems today as though it is a giant bird with its neck stretched to the blue sky – and the sky *is* blue today.

465. They take the lift to the third level, as high as clouds if there were clouds. As high as sky. Below them all the world looks lost in a blue haze. 'Breathe,' says the woman of the blue flowers and she presses his hand in hers. 'Breathe,' she says again, 'you are not cutting cloth.' Hayyim snatches for breath.

466. Michelle does not answer her phone or buzz me into her stair when I call at her street door. I knock till the concierge of the building hears. He asks me where's the fire and he chuckles to himself. I explain to him that Michelle is not answering her phone or her door and she has not been selling blue postcards or books or CDs at the foot of the Eiffel Tower for above a week. I tell him I am worried.

467. Yves Klein married Rotraut Uecker on 21 January 1962. He had wanted to stage the event on 20 January, which was the feast day of St Sebastian, a symbolically charged day for Klein after he had been made a Knight of the Order of the Archers in 1957. But the Order had strict

rules against holding a wedding on this sacred day and so it had to be on 21 January. The invitations, as you might expect, were printed in gold, blue and pink.

468. Pageboys wore International Klein Blue (IKB) bow ties.

469. His mother wore a dress in International Klein Blue (IKB).

470. The bride and groom departed the church in a white Jaguar filled with blue and white flowers.

471. It was such a blue spectacle, a work of performance art. Yves Klein was disappointed to discover the next day that his wedding did not get even a mention in any of the newspapers.

472. The concierge shakes his keys in the air and he suggests we go check on her apartment. He is a small man. Neatly dressed with an orange cravat tucked into the neck of his shirt. He walks with a pronounced limp, his left foot dragging a little. We take the lift to Michelle's floor. He unlocks her front door – which is blue. Nothing inside looks amiss.

473. Hayyim breathes and he says to the woman of the blue flowers that he has decided on a wish.

He says it is everything and nothing and he laughs at the joke he has made, though maybe he is the only one who understands it.

474. On 13 May 1962 the artist Franz Kline died. Joan Miró penned a note of condolence and sent it off to the artist's wife, except he made a mistake and it was sent to Mrs Yves Klein – Rotraut Uecker – instead. The envelope was edged in a dark blue.

475. Yves Klein laughed at Miró's mistake and wrote to assure the artist that he was in rude good health. As fit as a fiddle. Blue-sky happy and looking forward to being a father very soon.

476. Michelle's flat is empty of her things. It is as though she never was. As though we'd never lain down together on the bed or sat drinking coffee at her kitchen table. All the swallows on the telephone wires outside her window are gone and the pictures of the swallows on the wall, too – all except that first Dalí picture with the blue splashed ink that is somehow also a swallow. That picture she has left and there is meaning in that.

477. 'Sorry,' says the concierge with the orange cravat and he does exactly the same thing then with his hands that the man at the stall near

the Eiffel Tower had done. He locks his thumbs together and flaps his fingers as though he has created a bird. Then that bird he has made flies away over his shoulder and, in the dropping of his hands, disappears. The sky behind him has lost its blue.

478. Hayyim leans out over the edge, feels the press of the air against his chest. The woman of the blue flowers knows his wish without him having told her. She squeezes reassurance into his hand with hers and together they leap into the void.

479. On 15 May 1962 Yves Klein fell sick. His doctors said he should rest but he said he had work to do. There were blue paintings to finish. He would be a father in one not faraway day and so there was work to be done. He shut himself in his studio and, his mind all in a fever, he busied himself with art.

480. Of course Michelle has flown – she was only a summer-visiting swallow after all. An invention of my imagination. The one that never was, rewritten as a fiction so that an old man could love and be loved as he once wanted to be. And now she has gone and the sky is only a memory of blue, but it is no heartbreak, is nothing more than waking from a dream.

481. The concierge shrugs and he ushers me from the room, his hands pushing the air against me like he is shooing away chickens or cats. He locks the blue door to Michelle's apartment and we take the elevator back to the ground floor. He sees me to the front door and locks it behind me.

482. The air seems to hold him and the woman of the blue flowers reminds him to breathe again and together they seem to be held by nothing at all – by God, her God and his God. 'Everything and nothing,' Hayyim says again.

483. Yves Klein was at work on another triptych of sponge reliefs. He was using blue and pink and gold. He had a studio in the rue Campagne-Première. The studio was fairly rudimentary and without proper ventilation.

484. The handling of the chemicals that kept the pigment true for all time was fairly toxic – see an International Klein Blue (IKB) painting today and it is just as blue as it was when it left Yves Klein's studio. Not much was known about its toxicity then. Yves Klein, already sick, was breathing in dangerous amounts of these toxic chemicals.

485. His name is printed in the next day's news-papers, though in the papers Hayyim is again called Henri. It is a record of his death. The statements of bystanders were written down in the blue notebooks of the gendarmes. They said he did not look unhappy and his jumping from the Eiffel Tower was unexpected. He was talking to himself, they said and they said maybe he was joyously mad.

486. It was 6 June 1962. The report said his pockets were filled with feathers that spilled out on to the ground when he fell. They said he was a tailor and they said he was a Jew. Round his finger was wound a twisted blue thread. They did not say what this was for; they did not, any one of them, know. Nor was there any mention of a woman who jumped with him.

487. The next day there were blue flowers placed at Hayyim's shop door. The same blue flowers that had been placed there when he was taking a holiday from tailoring and everyone thought him dead – only now, everyone knew that he was.

488. You can lie in art and you can rewrite memory but truth is something that should be sacred and unchangeable like International Klein Blue (IKB). The dead swallow I held in the cup of

my two hands and I breathed on its feathered cheeks, it did not come back to life as I told Michelle. I know that even though I remember it the way I told her. The truth is that the dead never come back like that.

489. And in the end we are the voices of the dead, all the voices they have, we who live and love and laugh. We are the guardians of their truth and even in what we invent there should be truth. There *was* a blue postcard for sale at the foot of the Eiffel Tower and I *did* purchase it for only small money and it bore a blue stamp that was blank and franked 14 May 1957. And that *is* my birthday.

490. But there was no girl who sold me that blue card.

491. And, though there was a girl once and she did that thing with her hair and her eyes were blue flecked with honeycomb or gold, her name was not Michelle. And sitting here drinking tea from my Royal Copenhagen teacup with its handle too small for my fingers, and milk poured from a pink-and-blue-flowered Limoges *pot à lait* and sugar spooned from a blue willow pattern bowl with a chip in the rim, I remember that I once loved that girl and wished in vain that she loved me. So you see there is truth in there somewhere and lies there can be also.

492. On 6 June 1962 Yves Klein called his doctor to say he was unwell. It was a Paris summer day and the sky was blue and without his signature that day.

493. By the time the doctor arrived it was too late. Yves Klein suffered a heart attack and died – his lips at the end were blue. He was thirty-four years old, which was the same age as a man called Henri or Hayyim who leaped to his death from the top of the Eiffel Tower.

494. Today we remember Yves Klein for the blue that he patented – or he did not patent. We remember the *Leap into the Void* and an empty room that he convinced people was art and blue monochrome paintings all the same size but for sale at different prices.

495. We don't remember Henri or Hayyim and his leap into the blue. And perhaps we should. History should not be rewritten but it should also not be forgotten. There is no lie in what happened to Hayyim's father and mother and grandfather and we should remember that.

496. Yves Klein is buried beside his mother, Marie Raymond, and his aunt Rose, Tantine, in a cemetery in La Colle-sur-Loup in southern

France. There are always blue flowers placed on his grave.

497. And Michelle – or the girl she once was, the blue-eyed girl who tucked her hair so beautifully behind one ear? She is old now, I think.

498. I saw her picture once. I downloaded it from the internet. She was wearing a blue dress and her hair was the same as it is in memory – and on one side she had tucked it behind one ear – and maybe her eyes were the same, too.

499. She was smiling in the picture, a little out of focus and softly blue, but smiling all the same, and so I think she must be happy. It is enough that she is and enough that I remember her in Michelle. My father nods and smiles and I feel the press of his hand on my back.

500. And the man at the foot of the steps at *Le Passage de la Sorcière* in Montmartre – he is real, too. With his three chased silver egg cups and a wooden ball the size of a pea that he makes appear and disappear so you do not believe in truth but for a moment believe in lies – and you pay him for that. I can assure you that even the blue lapis stone in his tooth is real.

Acknowledgements

Thanks to my family for putting up with me as a writer. Thanks to 'The Demon Beaters of Lumb' for their unflagging positive support. Thanks to Urška Vidoni at Fairlight Books for picking up my submission and for her keen editorial eye in processing the novella and her diligent support at every step of the way; and thanks to copyeditor Phil Kelly who made the text much better than it was. Thanks to Fairlight Books for taking a chance with *Blue Postcards*.

Bookclub and writers' circle notes for the
Fairlight Moderns can be found at
www.fairlightmoderns.com

Share your thoughts about the
book with #BluePostcards

Also in the Fairlight Moderns series

JT TORRES

Taking Flight

When Tito is a child, his grandmother teaches
him how to weave magic around the ones
you love in order to keep them close.

She is the master and he is the pupil, exasperating
Tito's put-upon mother who is usually the focus of
their mischief.

As Tito grows older and his grandmother's mind
becomes less sound, their games take a dangerous
turn. They both struggle with a particular spell, one
that creates an illusion of illness to draw in love.
But as the lines between magic and childish tales
blur, so too do those between fantasy and reality.

'Taking Flight *is finely crafted,
lyrical song of a book.'*
—Amy Kurzweil, author of *Flying
Couch: a graphic memoir*

*'The exquisite writing of JT Torres is on full
display in this deftly told and spellbinding tale.'*
—Don Rearden, author of
The Raven's Gift

LOREE WESTRON

Missing Words

Postal worker Jenny's life is in the doldrums: her daughter all grown up and moving out, and her marriage falling apart. So, when a postcard from Australia marked 'insufficient address' lands on her sorting table, she does the unthinkable. On reading that the sender is begging the recipient for forgiveness and seeking reconciliation – and knowing it will never get delivered in time – she slips it up her sleeve and decides to deliver it herself.

Will Jenny be able to give the star-crossed lover the happy ending she feels that, somehow, she's lost?

'A tender and wise understanding
of the human condition.'
—Gabrielle Kimm, author of *His Last Duchess*

'Loree Westron writes with a subtle
beauty that made me catch my breath.'
—Laura Pearson, author of
I Wanted You To Know